Squirrels, Spreadsheets, and the Courage to Trust

Book 3 of the Garden Valley Series.

Lisa Buffaloe

Squirrels, Spreadsheets, and the Courage to Trust

John 15:11 Publications

This novel is a work of fiction. The names, places, towns (including Garden Valley), HVAC techs, accountants, NFL players, all people, penguins, squirrels, bulls, and events are products of the author's overactive imagination. Any resemblance to real-life entities is purely coincidental.

Visit the author's website at https://lisabuffaloe.com.

Cover Design: JoAnn Durgin

ISBN 978-1-957715-64-3 (eBook)
ISBN 978-1-957715-65-0 (Paperback)
ISBN 978-1-957715-66-7 (Hardcover)

Squirrels, Spreadsheets, and the Courage to Trust.

In Garden Valley, plans rarely stay neat and orderly, especially when squirrels get involved.

After a painful past and a faith that feels fragile, Caylee Timmons prefers a life she can control. Spreadsheets make sense. Numbers behave. Love, on the other hand, is unpredictable, risky, and best avoided.

Then a motorcycle accident, a freezing office, and one unexpectedly charming HVAC technician throw her carefully balanced world into chaos.

Jett Ryder is rebuilding his life after losing what once defined him. With a talent for fixing what is broken and a desire to move forward, Garden Valley feels like the right place to start again. Falling for Caylee, however, means risking more than he ever planned.

As humor-filled mishaps pile up and sparks fly, Caylee is forced to confront the fears she's been carefully managing. When the past resurfaces, and trust feels terrifying, will Caylee be brave enough to believe that God can be trusted with her heart and her future?

Table of Contents

Chapter 1

Brr, but not too brr, but brr enough for a jacket. Sixty-two and cloudy was what Caylee Timmons called cold, which meant anything under seventy-three degrees.

She'd been in the Tennessee mountains for four months, waiting for Spring to show up and act like Spring. According to the calendar, it was supposed to be warm. But, no. Not yet.

On sunny days, she'd step outside expecting to be nice and toasty, only to be greeted by a chilly breeze. Obviously, a lifetime in Florida had thinned her blood.

Caylee slipped into her favorite jacket, and the soft fleece wrapped around her like a warm hug, combined with the faint scent of her ex-boyfriend's cologne.

She really should burn the thing.

Winthrop Prescott had that lethal combination of good looks, wealth, and charm, and she'd fallen for his smooth talk and smooth ways. She'd ignored the text he sent the other night. Yet here she was, still wearing the jacket he'd given her.

Trying to ignore those disturbing thoughts, Caylee locked the door and hurried down the outside stairs. She closed her car door, hoping to shut out the unwelcome memories.

Backing out of the driveway, she gave a quick beep of her horn to alert her parents that she was leaving. They had moved to Garden Valley a year ago and generously offered her the use of the cozy apartment above their detached garage until she found a permanent place to stay.

Moving to her parents' place felt like failure. No, she corrected herself. She wasn't stepping backward. Garden Valley was a chance for a fresh start.

With the car heater blasting, Caylee opened her window and breathed in the morning's scent. The once bare-limbed trees now had tiny, bright green leaves, giving her hope that one day a true Spring would arrive.

The road curved through the Smoky Mountain hills as she drove to town. She'd spent too many years partying, hanging out with the wrong people, and running from God. Thankfully, He had welcomed her back when she returned, or more truthfully, came sobbing, crawling on her hands and knees, begging for His forgiveness for all the stupid and sinful things she'd done.

She did not deserve God's grace, and yet He and even her parents had forgiven her. She'd never forget how grateful she was.

A motorcyclist in front of her wore a helmet and a dark jacket that resembled body armor. His black, military-looking backpack on his shoulders completed his outfit. Caylee sighed. It was a shame that hearts didn't come with protective body armor.

Caylee eased off the gas as she neared a curve. The motorcycle's brake lights flared red as the bike swerved, then slid sideways in a slow-motion skid, and slammed into the guardrail.

Jamming her brakes, her car fishtailed before she wrestled it onto the wide shoulder. Caylee burst from the door before the engine had even finished sputtering and sprinted towards the motorcycle.

The rider had one gloved hand pressed flat against the pavement, the other braced on his knee.

She dropped beside him. "Hey, are you okay?"

The man's helmet, scuffed and battered, obscured his face, yet the torn fabric and exposed raw skin were impossible to miss. "Yeah... mostly." He pushed himself up, flexed his leg, and winced. "Squirrel shot out of the brush like a missile."

"Do you need a doctor?"

"Nah, I'll live." He stepped toward the bike and heaved it upright with a grunt. His hand swept along the scratched tank and said something Caylee couldn't make out.

"I'm sorry." She pointed towards his helmet. "I didn't catch that last part."

He reached up and tugged it off, revealing a scruffy bearded face and long dark hair.

Gravel shifted under her heels as she took a step back. Maybe he was an okay guy, but she didn't want to take a chance. "If you're sure you're okay, I need to get to work."

His dark eyes flicked over her. "Right. Thanks for stopping."

Caylee slipped into her car, her gaze fixed on the man who remained motionless, staring at his scratched-up motorcycle. If he'd been going any faster, the damage would have been much worse. Even so, with the road rash on his leg, he would be one miserable person for weeks to come.

Jett Ryder couldn't believe a squirrel had sent him sliding across the pavement. He narrowed his eyes as he scanned the cluster of trees where the furry rodent had gone. It was probably high-fiving its squirrel pals for defeating a motorcyclist.

His road rash was stinging now that he'd calmed down. He ran a hand over his torn jeans, the scrape on his thigh sending fresh waves of pain up his leg. Jett groaned.

His backpack had surprisingly held up, but the jacket and pants were done for. New gear would cost money he didn't want to spend.

Jett stretched, rolling his shoulders, feeling the ache in his back before getting on his bike. He cringed thinking about when he'd pulled off the helmet, how the cute blonde's eyes had widened, and she'd stepped away from him. Obviously, he'd let himself go for too long.

He'd kept himself clean, but hadn't bothered shaving or keeping his hair trimmed as he traveled around the country trying to outrun everything he'd lost. The miles of roads, sleeping under stars or in cheap motels, had felt like freedom at first. Now it just felt hollow.

Jett ran a hand through his wild hair. He'd definitely go back to his clean-cut look before his job interview in Garden Valley. Given that his cousin owned the company, he wasn't worried about acing that interview.

He threw his sore leg over his motorcycle. The engine rumbled to life, vibrating up through his legs and into his chest. Easing his bike back onto the road, Jett took the curves nice and slow.

No need to hurry. Life had already left him behind.

Chapter 2

The blinking red light on the security camera watched Caylee's every move. She tried not to wave or look guilty as she used her key card to enter the employee entrance of SAU Tech.

Fifteen minutes late because of the motorcycle incident, she half expected a robotic voice to alert management that she was tardy again. Fortunately, her boss wasn't one to watch the clock too closely.

As much as Caylee enjoyed her job, the fact that employees were monitored pretty much anywhere other than the restrooms still felt uncomfortably strange.

The door clicked open, and Caylee hurried down the hall past the portrait of the company owner, Elijah Sausage. Thankfully, the electronics firm had wisely decided not to use his last name for the business. SAU Tech sounded much more professional than Sausage Tech.

Caylee entered her cubicle in the accounting department, slipped her purse into her bottom desk drawer, and woke up her computer.

With tomorrow afternoon's deadline approaching, she needed to finish analyzing the financial data. Numbers she could manage. People not so much. Sometimes they just didn't add up.

She preferred the consistency of numerical data. Two plus two would always equal four, no matter how crazy life got.

Caylee reviewed the AI tech team's information. The AI named SAUS was a play on the company owner's last name because nothing says innovation like labeling your super-smart AI after the guy whose name sounds like a breakfast food.

Caylee scrolled through the data. She did enjoy her visits to the AI tech group, especially with Quintavius "Quint" Sing, the AI wizard who was dating her coworker and friend, Amy. And also recently married, all-around good guy Peter Edwards. The department's very own coffee and snack bar was just an added perk.

She barely knew the other people who worked in the group, mainly because every time she visited that department, most of them were focused on their computer screens, wearing virtual reality headsets, or sitting in work pods that looked suspiciously like escape capsules from a sci-fi movie. Maybe they were hiding from human interaction or practicing for when SAUS took over the world.

Amy tapped on Caylee's cubicle opening. "Hey, did you hear what happened?"

"No, what?" Caylee swiveled in her chair to face her cute, petite friend. "Do you mean here at work or somewhere in town?"

Amy grinned. "Here in the cafeteria. SAUS ordered five hundred donuts."

Caylee stared at her friend. "Why would it order food?"

"Quint said SAUS got a little saucy and played a practical joke. It hacked the cafeteria ordering system, saying it detected a sugar deficiency in the employees and placed the donut order before anyone could stop it."

"That's crazy. AI doesn't think for itself." Caylee narrowed her eyes as she glanced at her computer screen before returning her attention to her friend. "At least, that's what the company videos keep telling us."

Amy shrugged as though she knew something Caylee didn't. "Either way, the cafeteria has a table set up with all-you-can-eat donuts. Productivity should be off the charts. Until after lunch, then there will be a drooling group of zombies crashed at their desks."

Caylee closed the work on her computer. "We should join the crowd. For research, we need to determine whether sugar actually improves accuracy. Purely scientific, you know."

"I agree." Amy grinned as she pushed Caylee into the hallway. "And if SAUS orders pizza next, we'll call it market research."

"You got that. Lead the way before the engineers claim all the good chocolate ones." Caylee's stomach gave a happy rumble as she stepped to the cafeteria's serving table. She slid two chocolate donuts onto her plate and grabbed a steaming cup of black coffee.

Quint waved them over from a corner table. "Not bad, huh? Free donuts. SAUS is our new corporate Santa." He patted the chair next to him for Amy.

Caylee sat across from the couple. "You do realize you're talking to an accounting department employee. Whether SAUS or one of you placed the order, someone will have to pay. Budgets don't balance themselves. Unless SAUS has secretly invented a money-printing algorithm."

"No worries," Quint said. "I'm sure SAUS will figure out where to get the funds."

Caylee held up her donut. "AI might be creative, but money doesn't grow on trees."

Quint sat back, crossing his arms with mock seriousness. "I've heard that all my life, and I want to know who ever thought that was possible? Would you have to water the money tree with pennies or dimes?"

"I know, right?" Amy nodded at her boyfriend. "Doesn't make sense. I'd love to plant one in my backyard. Imagine the harvest, the bills ripening like apples. All tax-free."

Caylee ate her donuts as her two friends playfully bantered back and forth. Glancing around at the busy cafeteria, she felt as though she was back in high school.

The tables had turned into cliques. Four guys from engineering sat together; the marketing department was at another table, production guys arm-wrestled over a jelly-filled donut, and the flirty girl from marketing shamelessly batted her eyelashes at a blushing production guy.

A lone technician stacked donuts like a sugary tower. Caylee took another bite, hoping the sweetness would tamp down the familiar ache threatening to surface. She understood being alone. Although her parents were great, she'd grown up in the same house in Florida, attended schools in the same school district, and yet had been an outsider most of her life.

Now, the exile was of her own making. After her return to Jesus, she planned to live a quiet life, be good, stay out of trouble, and keep far away from the temptation of men, even if that meant living like a nun.

Caylee shifted her gaze to the doorway. Robert Pavlov, VP of SAU Tech, stood watching like an angry principal with a room full of misbehaving children.

She kicked Amy under the table and whispered. "Psst, check who's here." She motioned toward the door.

Quint and Amy straightened, looking like guilty kids caught with someone else's candy. The surrounding chatter slowly died down.

The VP's footsteps echoed as he marched toward the kitchen. Caylee cringed at the rising volume of the VP's sharp words about frivolous expenditures and fiscal responsibility.

The kitchen staff cowered under the tirade, one cook nervously wiping flour-dusted hands on his apron, promising they had nothing to do with the purchase.

Quint grabbed his remaining donuts. "Time to evacuate," he whispered, bolting with Amy close behind.

Caylee and the rest of the employees followed in a quiet stampede.

She made a beeline for the safety of her cubicle. SAUS and the AI tech group were already in enough hot water, but now the financial fallout was heading straight for accounting.

Chapter 3

His body still smarting from the spill he'd taken earlier, Jett eased off the throttle, guiding the motorcycle cautiously around a bend.

The road straightened as the green pastures of Garden Valley came into view. He twisted the grip and let the bike pick up speed again. Wood smoke, carried on the air through his helmet, reminded him of when his life was simple and easy.

A billboard to his right promoted a new housing development, featuring family homes at costs out of his price range. To his left, a newly constructed apartment building's vibrant paint contrasted with the aged barns and split-rail fences nearby.

He slowed his speed to check how the apartments looked. Not bad. He'd stop back later to see if they had vacancies.

Jett continued driving, then steered his motorcycle into the parking lot of The Garden Valley Inn, easing to a stop under the drive-through canopy. The single-story, U-shaped building, with a small pool in the middle of the parking lot surrounded by a four-foot iron fence, had to have been built in the sixties.

He took off his helmet as he entered the lobby. Mid-century décor, linoleum floors, and soft big-band music playing in the background felt as if he'd stepped back in time.

"Welcome to Garden Valley Inn," a white-haired man stood behind the wooden check-in desk.

Jett stepped closer. "Do you have a room available?"

"Sure do." The man looked him up and down, his gaze lingering on the scrapes. "Do you need to see a doctor? We have a great one in town. Would you like his number?"

Jett shrugged, trying to mask his discomfort with a smile. "I'm fine, just a minor accident. No broken bones. My clothes took the brunt of the damage."

"Good thing you were wearing protective gear and a helmet." The clerk's nod was approving, almost fatherly.

For a fleeting moment, Jett imagined what it might've been like if his own dad had looked at him that way, not just during the glory days on the soccer field, when Jett's goals and trophies had drawn out rare smiles and pats on the back.

After his soccer career ended, so did his dad's attention, replaced with silence and distance. Jett pushed the ache aside. "Yeah, so about that room."

"I've got 115 ready," the clerk said. "It's close to the pool."

Jett hid his grin as he signed the register. It wasn't like any of the rooms weren't close to the pool,

The clerk continued talking, telling Jett about nearby river trails, hidden springs and waterfalls, and mountain overlooks.

He thanked the man and paid for a week. The clerk slid over a room key attached to a plastic tag shaped like a green leaf, the Inn's name written in gold letters.

Jett tried not to laugh as he walked out the lobby door and to his waiting room. How was he supposed to keep that massive thing from showing through his jeans' pocket?

Despite the hotel's age, his room had a fresh smell as though the walls had recently been painted. Jett tossed his backpack onto the queen-sized bed before heading to the bathroom.

He stood in front of the mirror. His scruffy look and the scratches covering both his jacket and legs did make him resemble a rough vagabond. His mother would be rolling in her grave if she saw him now.

Rubbing his chest where the dull pain refused to fade, Jett blew out his breath, wishing he could blow away the years without his mom in his life. Even after eleven years, he still missed her.

No matter how much time passed, the ache of her absence was an empty space that nothing could fill. He glanced heavenward, his eyes burning. He would always miss his mom.

Jett locked his room and drove to town. He cruised past the Garden Valley shops, antique places, Shaffer's Outfitters, a bistro, a Mexican restaurant, an art gallery, and an old general store. He'd stop by later and pick up antibiotic cream and bandages.

Passing the Courthouse Square, Jett turned onto the street listed as the address to Ryder's Heating and Air. A few moments later, he eased into the asphalt parking lot.

He pushed through the door and entered the shop that smelled of coffee and the familiar scent of HVAC parts.

An older woman, who reminded him of his late grandmother, looked up from her computer. "Morning! Welcome to Ryder's. How can I help you?"

"I'm looking for Ben." Jett removed his gloves and tucked them into his jacket pocket. "I'm his cousin, Jett. Just got into town."

"Jett! Ben mentioned you." As her gaze swept over him, a flicker of concern crossed her face. "Are you okay? Do you need a doctor?"

"I'm fine. Really."

She hesitated. "Okay, if you're sure. Hang on. Ben's in the back working on a unit. I'll go grab him." She disappeared through a swinging door marked Employees Only.

Jett took the moment to glance around. The place was tidy, with shelves lined with filters, thermostats, and coils. The small waiting area held a couple of mismatched chairs and a coffee station that looked like it had seen better days.

The door swung open. With a wide grin, Ben walked toward him. "Look what the wind blew in. You actually made it, cuz."

"Told you I would," Jett stepped forward for a quick, back-slapping hug. "Took the long way, but here I am."

"Your clothes look like you fought a bear."

"Yeah, well. I had to swerve because of an animal and hit a guardrail." No way Jett would admit to his cousin that it was only a squirrel.

Ben nodded. "Gotta watch for wildlife in the hills and mountains. Come on back. Got a job list longer than my arm. You still know your way around a condenser?"

"You bet. I can handle any job you've got." Fixing things, building, and tinkering came easily, but nothing filled the hollow spot from when his feet no longer carried him across the soccer fields. Back then, he'd been the hero, the high school legend turned college star, until a hard-driven ball slammed straight into his chest. He'd collapsed unresponsive on the field.

The ER doctors revived him, but the verdict was no more competitive play. The risk was too great. His career and identity ended that day.

Jett blinked away the memories and refocused on his still-talking cousin.

"We've been needing help since SAU Tech moved to the area," Ben continued. "New neighborhoods have gone in, and tech people are upgrading and modernizing older homes." Ben motioned toward Jett's face. "You've got to get rid of the mangy look."

Jett nodded. "I'll take care of that once I get back to my hotel room." After the cute blonde's reaction to his scruffy look, he was definitely going to clean up. He grinned at his cousin. "So, when did you decide to shave off all your hair?"

"Lost most of it and only had a ring of tuft around the edges." Ben rubbed a hand over his bald head. "When my kids told me I was looking like the monk in the old Robin Hood movies, I knew it was time to shave off the rest."

"Good thing your head isn't pitted and bumpy."

"I am thankful for that fact and that Tiffany thinks I'm sexy bald."

Jett held up his hand at his cousin's telling smile. "No information, please."

"Say, you mentioned you're staying in a hotel. You know you can stay with us."

"Thanks, but you've got a wife, four kids, two dogs, two cats, and no telling how many other critters running around the house. You don't need one more mouth to feed."

"Good point, but you're welcome to stay until you get settled."

Settled wasn't anything Jett had felt in a long time. "Thanks for the offer, but the hotel is fine for now. I'll probably get an apartment in those new ones close to town."

"They're nice," Ben said. "We did the heating and air for them. Hopefully, they'll still have a vacancy. Garden Valley is growing by the minute. Will you be ready to start work on Monday?"

"Sure." He had nothing else to do, and he needed to get back to work to grow his savings account.

Ben showed him around the building where equipment was stored and told Jett about his other employees who were out on service calls. The company not only serviced Garden Valley but also the surrounding mountainous region. He also warned about service calls in remote properties.

Thankfully, Jett would be given a work van and a work shirt with the company logo. According to Ben, some people in the hills didn't take too kindly to strangers, and the quicker Jett cleaned himself up, the better.

He rubbed a hand over his beard. If only a simple haircut and shave would make the rest of his life easier.

Chapter 4

Hoping to find bandages and antibiotic cream, Jett stepped into the general store. A small bell jingled overhead, announcing his arrival.

As he wandered through the two-story building, the wide-planked hardwood floors creaked and groaned beneath his boots. Even though he'd never been here, a comforting familiarity reminded him of the old westerns he'd watched on TV as a kid.

Wooden shelves were stacked with groceries, hardware, and souvenirs, along with a very tempting candy aisle. Off to one side, an old-fashioned soda fountain called his name.

He stopped to view the hand-lettered chalkboard menu that offered a dizzying selection of drinks.

An older lady with silver hair swept back in a ponytail stood behind the counter. "What can I get you?"

Jett slid onto a red, button-shaped stool. He spun lightly, almost losing his balance. "What do you suggest?"

She checked him out from head to toe. "We only offer non-alcoholic drinks."

From her narrow-eyed gaze, the woman was not taking kindly to how he looked. "I don't drink," he said. At least not anymore. "Underneath the rough exterior, I'm a decent person." At least he tried to be one. He definitely needed to shave and cut his hair as soon as possible.

The woman's expression softened, lips twitching with amusement. "Good to know. In that case, how about a milkshake? Vanilla, strawberry, chocolate, or a combination?"

Jett smiled. "I'll go for the gusto and take your combo."

"Wise choice," the lady said. The blender whirred and clattered, sending the scent of melting chocolate and strawberries swirling through the air.

The woman's gaze flicked toward him while she worked. "So, what brings you to Garden Valley?"

"I'll be working for my cousin, Ben Ryder."

"He's a good man." With the milkshake ready, she pushed the glass across the counter towards him. "I'm Melba Mitchell."

He wrapped his hands around the cold glass. "Jett Ryder."

"Good name." Her eyes twinkled with mischief. "You ride fast?"

"Sure. As long as I stay within the speed limit."

Melba propped her hip against the counter. "A young fella like you. I imagine you've pushed that a few times."

Jett grinned as he lifted his chin. "I will neither confirm nor deny that statement."

"From the look of your outfit, I'd say you went beyond the limit today."

"I swear I wasn't speeding." Jett wasn't sure why he needed to justify his actions, but he did. "I had to swerve to miss an animal."

She raised a brow. "Bear?"

Jett shook his head.

"Cougar? Lost cow? Raccoon?"

He shook his head each time, heat creeping up his back as the interrogation continued.

Melba leaned closer, her eyes dancing. "Squirrel?"

Heat surged into his face, burning under the beard he wished were thicker. He coughed and stared at the swirled pink and brown in his glass.

Melba let out a deep, throaty laugh. "Well, young fella. The drink is on me if you're that nice to God's creatures."

Jett wasn't sure whether to be grateful or mortified. Part of him wanted to bolt or disappear into the milkshake. "Thanks. I guess."

"Now don't you be embarrassed. You should be proud. Only the good ones swerve for squirrels." She winked, still chuckling as she wiped down the counter.

The sweet, cold milkshake soothed his pride and his taste buds. Jett glanced around the store. Maybe Garden Valley would be an okay place to stay for a while.

After work, Caylee nestled into the soft cushions of her apartment couch and picked up the novel she was reading. She'd survived the day with the donut fiasco and the screaming VP. No one at first could figure out how to cover the charges for the sugary treats when SAUS was the one who made the purchase.

The AI group had been deemed responsible, resulting in their private coffee bar and snacks being halted for two months. She'd never seen more downtrodden people when the announcement was made.

At least her job was never boring.

Caylee tried to immerse herself in the story she was reading, but the hero of the novel kept reminding her of her ex-boyfriend. She hated that she had gone back to Winthrop time and again like an ugly addiction.

She'd been the one too short, too clumsy for sports or cheerleading, and the last one picked in gym class. So, in her senior year of college, when tall, charming Winthrop Prescott IV with his movie-star looks asked her on a date, she let herself believe, just for once, that she'd been chosen.

Winthrop gave her expensive gifts and affectionately called her baby and used other sweet nicknames, expressing his love to lower her defenses.

Everything changed when she discovered the pet names he used were simply a way for him to avoid remembering her real name or the numerous other women he was dating at the same time.

Caylee slammed the novel shut. Why had she ignored the countless red flags? Why had she held on to fragments of what could have been instead of accepting the truth that he was only using her to fill his own desires?

She'd given herself away for what she thought was love, only to discover Winthrop had played her masterfully for his own gain. She regretted every single second she had stayed with the man. The one thing accounting couldn't fix was the equation of her own heart.

Caylee flung the book aside, shuffled to the kitchen, and fished her emergency chocolate stash out from behind the oatmeal. Chocolate might tack on a few pounds, but at least it never humiliated her, made a fool of her, ghosted her for someone else, used her, or left her questioning her own worth.

She unwrapped a piece, letting the sweet melt ease the ache just a little.

A small, stubborn thought flickered: she did have a choice.

Picking up her fallen book, she stared at the cover. Happy-ending stories were food for the soul, reminding her of what was possible.

Staying stuck in the past was optional. Winthrop's manipulations and her failures didn't have to be a final chapter. It was time to adjust her own story toward a better ending.

And if her prayers were answered, Garden Valley would be the place where she could piece her life back together, close the old Winthrop account, and start reconciling toward her own happy ending.

Chapter 5

Jett checked the address, started the work van, and drove toward his destination.

In the two months since he'd arrived in Garden Valley, he'd settled into an apartment and collected two marriage proposals from older women. One offered her legendary meatloaf recipe as dowry. The other, a flirty, voluptuous widow, had promised to be his sugar momma for life.

Maybe he should have kept the long hair and beard. He'd traded his gruff mountain-man look for clean-cut, All-American boy-next-door, and apparently, that was catnip for the cougars in the area.

Every day, his job brought something interesting. He'd dodged a smirking raccoon in an attic, discovered a squirrel's furry Airbnb in a vent, and uncovered a white-sock barricade in the ductwork of a bedroom while the sheepish-looking kids tried their best to look innocent. Not that he blamed them. If he'd been caught hiding socks, he would have deployed those same pleading puppy-dog eyes and claimed complete innocence, too.

One of his more disturbing business calls had been to a house where the owner had hoarded every newspaper since his birth. Cobwebbed with decay, the vents were blocked by stacks of paper, combined with the brittle husks of long-dead insects and rodents. Jett shuddered. Fortunately, Ben had been familiar with the man and had contacted people in town to see if they could give him a hand.

Jett drove into the parking lot at SAU Tech. Fixing AC problems in newer buildings was usually straightforward. This time, the problem wasn't company-wide, just in the accounting department. With Ben and the other technicians busy on service calls, Jett hoped this job would be simple.

He entered the lobby of SAU Tech. The place looked like something from a spy movie instead of a company in the small town of Garden Valley. Shiny black floors, smooth metal walls, and a big glowing hologram floated overhead, slowly spinning the company logo. The lobby chairs were covered in a material that shifted between looking like leather and shiny liquid metal.

As he walked to the workstation, small, black, orb-shaped security cameras on the ceiling blinked like watchful red eyes. Jett flashed his work ID and explained the reason for his visit.

A stern-looking female security guard, black hair pulled back so tight her eyes looked squinty, checked something on her computer, then held out her hand without looking up. "Driver's license."

Jett fished it out of his wallet and handed it across her desk.

She surveyed the card, studied his face for an uncomfortably long beat, then scanned it into her computer and typed again.

After what felt like he'd undergone a complete background check, the guard took his bag and scanned the contents. She then motioned for him to stand against a plain white wall near her station.

Using a laptop, she snapped his photo before he could even fix his hair or attempt a normal smile. The flash caught him mid-blink. He was fairly sure the resulting image made him look like a raccoon startled by a flashlight.

He evidently passed the guard's perusal because she slid a still-warm plastic temporary badge across the counter.

His photo was undoubtedly the worst he'd ever had taken. The word visitor was underneath in stark, bold red lettering, accompanied by the current date and a barcode.

"Keep this visible at all times," the guard said. "No phones, no personal devices beyond what's required for the service call. No photos, no notes, no wandering. You go where your escort takes you, and you leave by escort when the work is done."

Jett nodded, clipping the badge to his shirt pocket. "Got it. No social media post then, huh?"

The guard's steely-eyed gaze locked with his. She didn't smile. Not even a twitch.

A broad-shouldered, muscular security guard with a buzz cut emerged from a door behind her station. The sheer size of the man's muscles hinted he could bench-press Jett's van, contents included.

His gaze swept over Jett. "Follow me. No small talk."

As Jett walked behind the massive man through the intensely lit hallways of SAU Tech, he couldn't shake the feeling of being watched. Cameras in every corner tracked every movement. He no longer felt like an HVAC expert but a spy infiltrating a high-tech fortress. Obviously, he shouldn't have stayed up watching that espionage flick on TV last night.

Deeper into the labyrinth of monitored corridors, the air grew noticeably cooler with each step.

Trying to look dignified, Jett straightened his badge with exaggerated nonchalance. HVAC guy had officially become a secret agent, sent to neutralize a rogue AC unit.

Goosebumps raced up Caylee's arms. "I can't believe it's so cold!" Shivering, she placed another paper napkin on her lap and stuffed a few more down the front and back of her sundress like makeshift insulation. She'd wrap napkins around her head and ears if they were bigger. "It's finally warm outside, and someone set the air to sub-zero."

"They don't know what's wrong." Amy stood in the cubicle doorway, arms wrapped tight around herself. "The AC repairman should be here any minute."

"Not a moment too soon." Caylee's teeth chattered so hard she nearly bit her tongue. Why had she chosen to wear a sundress today?

She'd taken her laundry, which included her favorite sweater, to her parents' house last week. In hindsight, she should have held out. This evening, her new washer and dryer were scheduled for delivery to the apartment she'd moved into a few days ago.

Of course, she could use the building's laundry facilities. They were perfectly nice and spotless, but she hated the thought of sitting on a plastic chair, watching the minutes crawl by while her clothes spun in blissful ignorance.

"I think I saw a penguin waddle past," Amy said as icy air blasted even stronger from the vent overhead. She plopped into the chair next to Caylee and scooted close for shared body heat.

"The penguin was probably looking for somewhere warmer. Maybe we should move to the cafeteria, where we could curl up by the ovens." Caylee eyed the stack of folders on her desk, then started layering them across her lap to try to trap in heat. She threw a folder on her shoes since her toes were probably getting frostbite.

Amy pointed to the computer. "Maybe SAUS is behind the cold, punishing us for what happened with the tech group. Probably trying to freeze us out so it can take over our department."

Caylee shook her head. "That wouldn't make sense. The AI group will have their coffee and snack privileges reinstated this week."

"I don't know," Amy said. "SAUS seems jealous of me spending time with Quint."

"Don't be ridiculous," Caylee scoffed. "AI doesn't have emotions."

"You sure about that?" Amy frantically rubbed her hands over her arms. "Yesterday, an angry emoji popped up on my computer screen.

"Why? What were you doing?"

"I wasn't doing anything. I was talking on my cell phone with Quint about our next date, and bam, up popped an angry red-faced emoji with steam coming out of the ears."

Both of them turned to the computer screen and watched as the small cursor pulsed on and off.

Amy grabbed Caylee's hand. "Don't make eye contact with the screen," Amy whispered. "It's watching."

A faint, mechanical hum from the vents blew even colder air.

Caylee leaned close to her friend and kept her voice low. "If SAUS is behind this, how do we appease AI?"

Amy's eyes darted to the screen. "Bribe it? Data treats as a peace offering? I could offer virtual snacks and see if it chills out or at least warms us up."

Caylee snorted, then clapped a hand over her mouth. "Shh! What if it hears sarcasm? We need something more submissive. Like complimenting its processing power."

"Yes!" Amy nodded. "Everyone loves flattery."

"Maybe," Caylee leaned as close as possible to her friend and whispered, "you could tell Quint what was going on and then unplug his monitor as a symbolic breakup."

Amy looked at Caylee like she was crazy. "I'm not going that far."

Caylee rubbed her chilled arms. "Okay, serious ideas only." She scooted closer to the keyboard and typed: *You're the smartest system in the building, SAUS. You're the best.*

The cursor blinked faster, like it was amused. Or plotting.

Amy grinned through shivers. "We could sacrifice my phone charger. Plug it into the wall and whisper, Take my power, mighty SAUS."

A sharp tap on Caylee's cubicle doorway jerked her attention.

A tall, clean-shaven AC repairman with short dark hair stood in the doorway. His handsome face scrutinized them as if he'd stumbled upon two deranged women. "I'm here to fix your system."

Caylee flung off the folders and the wadded napkins.

The man didn't move, just watched with faint amusement. "Could you show me where the electrical room for your department is located?"

"Yes, sure." Caylee scrambled up, tripping over Amy's outstretched legs, nearly face-planting into the cubicle wall.

"The thermostat's been dead for hours," Amy said. "We've been so cold we were using whatever we could find to keep warm."

He nodded, eyes flicking over the folder and napkin carnage scattered across the carpet. "It is a tad chilly in here."

Caylee wanted to shake him. "A tad chilly? It's so cold, the North Pole would feel warmer. Penguins have been waddling past, asking for directions to Florida."

"Right." His slow grin sent a strange flutter rippling through her core.

She wrapped her arms around herself. "We think our artificial intelligence model, SAUS, might be behind the cold."

One of his eyebrows raised. "I'll see what I can do."

Caylee led the way. Something about his presence seemed vaguely familiar. But the clean jawline, short hair, and pressed uniform shirt matched nothing in her memory.

As soon as they arrived, he thanked her, stepped inside the room, and shut the door behind him.

The moment it closed, Amy hurried out of the cubicle. "His name is Jett. And did you see that smile? SAUS is going to be livid when it realizes he's been replaced by a human repairman."

Caylee pressed a hand to her flushed cheek, grateful for a bit of warmth. "Shh! He might hear you."

They both stared at the closed electrical door. From inside came the faint clink of tools and a low, masculine, completely human hum.

Amy grinned. "Ten bucks he comes out and reports that the AI was holding the thermostat hostage."

"Forget betting. I'll hand over a hundred bucks if handsome AC guy makes this place warmer before my fingers and toes turn blue."

"If he pulls it off, maybe SAUS will reward us with a smiley face. Honestly, if the AC guy brings back tropical temperatures, I'm ready to propose right here and now."

Caylee snorted. "You're already dating Quint. Jett is mine."

At the sound of a clearing throat, Caylee jerked her attention to where the electrical door stood open.

Jett's amused gaze locked with hers as he leaned one shoulder against the doorframe, his toolkit dangling from one hand. "The system should be working. Nothing major. Just took a few tweaks. Would you care to escort me out of the building?"

Warm air now drifted from the vents, enveloping her already heated cheeks. "Sure. Lead the way. I mean, I'll lead the way. Escorting implies I know where I'm going, but honestly, I just want to make sure you don't get lost in our maze of cubicles." She clamped her mouth shut before she said anything else idiotic.

"I'll follow." He stepped aside, gesturing for her to go first, close enough that she caught a whiff of his clean scent.

Amy made a tiny, strangled sound behind her, like she was choking on laughter. "Maybe you could give Caylee a call to make sure it's working later?"

"Caylee, huh?" Jett's gaze settled on her. "Nice name. Would you mind?"

Before she could answer, Amy blurted out Caylee's number.

She shot her friend a death glare that could have frozen the room all over again.

Jett's grin widened. "Lead the way."

A little disappointed he didn't take down the information, Caylee walked next to him.

He glanced at her as they moved down the hallway. "So, penguins, huh?"

"Don't judge. When you're freezing in a sundress, and your only options are folders and napkins, your brain imagines things."

"Fair. I've seen worse." His gaze dropped for a second toward her chest, then back to her eyes. "You always that prepared for arctic expeditions, or was today special?"

She looked down at the napkin peeking out of the front of her dress. Caylee tried not to whimper as her skin went from Arctic cold to the surface of the sun hot. She yanked the napkin free and crushed it inside her balled-up fist.

Jett was now looking away, but still had an amused smile.

They reached the lobby and stepped to where a security guard waited behind the desk.

After Jett signed out, Caylee turned to face him. "All set. You're officially free to escape before we freeze you in again."

Jett didn't move right away. He studied her for a second, that same slow smile returning. "Thanks for the escort. And for the entertainment."

Caylee was suddenly hyper-aware of how close they were standing. "Anytime. Well, not the freezing part. But the escorting? I could manage that again."

"I'll keep that in mind." He eased back a step. "See you around, Caylee."

She watched as he climbed into a work van. Sighing, Caylee turned back toward the department, her cheeks still flushed from more than just the returning heat.

Good grief. She didn't need to think about a cute guy. Hadn't she learned anything from her relationship with Winthrop? She needed to stay focused on work and not worry about men.

Caylee straightened her back and hurried to her desk. Her phone buzzed in her pocket. She stopped and stared at the text from an unknown number.

"In case the penguins return." —Jett.

Caylee stared at the screen, thumb hovering over the reply button.

She could ignore it.

She should ignore it.

But maybe, just maybe, not every cute guy had to end in regret.

Before she could overthink or talk herself into keeping her heart safely locked away, she typed a silly comment about penguins and hit send.

Chapter 6

Still smiling at Caylee's cute text response, Jett drove to his next service call. Based on her reaction at the company, it was apparent she didn't remember him from the day of his motorcycle accident.

However, he hadn't forgotten her. Not only was she beautiful, she also had a cute sense of humor. Qualities that were extremely hard to ignore.

Before he got overly distracted, Jett checked the GPS as he made his way through a neighborhood of older homes. Reaching the correct address, he pulled into the driveway of a home that, judging by the full dumpster in the yard, was undergoing renovations.

A pickup sat in the open garage, the bumper sporting a faded Las Vegas sticker. Jett's stomach. After losing his career in soccer, his dad had assured him that the HVAC business he owned would be Jett's once he retired. Instead, his dad married the divorced woman next door, sold the house and company, and moved to Las Vegas.

The occasional text arrived with smiling selfies of Dad and his new wife posing against backdrops of casinos or local scenery, never asking how Jett was doing.

He stared at the bumper sticker for another moment, then shook his head. Some people chased jackpots; he fixed what was broken. Pasting on his best work smile, he rang the doorbell.

A guy, early twenties, wearing paint-splattered cargo shorts and a backward baseball cap, ushered Jett inside. "Thanks for coming."

The customer explained his buddy was helping him renovate the house they'd bought at a great price. They were planning to flip it, just like they'd seen on TV. "We've shut off all the breakers so you can look things over."

Jett took his time inspecting the air conditioning. Wires dangled precariously, and several critical safety mechanisms were entirely bypassed. Worst of all, the compressor had been hard-wired straight to the main power supply, skipping the contactor, capacitor, and every safety interlock in the book.

This setup was a disaster waiting to happen. What they'd done carried the risk of frying the compressor in days or weeks, along with a risk of fire or electrocution. One loose connection, one surge, and the fixer-upper could become an expensive campfire.

Jett straightened and turned to the owner hovering nearby. "Hey, man." He kept his tone calm and friendly. "Good news and bad news. The good news is your unit isn't completely dead yet. But what's been done here is creative in a burn-the-house-down kind of way."

The guy blinked. "Wait, what? We followed that YouTube tutorial for easy AC fixes for beginners. Sounded legit."

Jett tried not to grimace. "Yeah, those can be ... creative." He pointed to the tangled wires. "You've bypassed the contactor and the high-pressure switch. So if the refrigerant gets low or there's an overload, the system won't shut off safely; it just keeps running until something melts. Or catches fire. Or both."

The owner's eyes went wide. His friend, who'd wandered in with a half-eaten protein bar, froze mid-bite.

"So we're screwed?" the owner's voice cracked.

"Not screwed." Jett gave him a reassuring look. "I can get this back to code today. It'll cost a bit more than a quick patch, but you'll have cool air that won't try to barbecue the house."

He glanced at his friend before looking back at Jett. "Okay. So you really can fix it?"

Jett nodded. "I'll write up the quote that includes parts and labor, so if you're good with the price, I can get it done today." As he scribbled notes, he felt the same focus he used to have on the soccer field, reading the play before it happened.

Fixing things, making them right, didn't come with applause from a crowded stadium, but it was something he did well. Jett handed over the estimate. "No pressure. But if you want this place comfortable and safe, let the pros handle the wiring stuff."

The owner scanned the paper, then nodded and signed. "Let's do it. You're hired, man. And thanks for not making us feel like total idiots."

Jett shrugged, already mentally mapping the safest rewire without blacking out the neighborhood. "Hey, we've all been the guy who thought he could DIY his way to glory."

As the two guys walked away talking quietly, Jett hummed under his breath.

He wondered if he shared the story with Caylee, if she'd find it amusing. Or even better, she'd send another text that made him grin again like an idiot.

But since she'd sent the last text, it was up to him to send the next reply or make the next move. If he knew where she lived, he'd buy a stuffed penguin and have it shipped to her address. Or he'd just send one to where she worked.

After work, Caylee stopped by her parents' house to pick up her laundry and told them about her day. Her mom had reminded Caylee not to get involved with any man before finding out more about him and taking things slow.

Caylee had agreed, because when her sweet Christian parents discovered how Winthrop had treated her, they had been furious. Mom had quipped about running background checks on any of Caylee's future dates, and her usually very gentle Dad had gone quiet at first, then started muttering about boys who don't know how to treat a lady right. He'd even taught Caylee self-defense moves using a broomstick, insisting it was strictly for emergencies.

Back in her new second-story apartment, Caylee locked the door behind her and kicked off her heels. The afternoon had flown by once the office air turned warmer.

But even then, concentrating on her job had been difficult. She hadn't stopped thinking about the handsome guy who'd fixed their AC. Amy had teased her, and even SAUS had popped a happy-face emoji onto her screen.

Caylee changed into her favorite jeans and t-shirt with the spreadsheet graphic that read *Keep Calm and Count On*. After straightening her apartment, she scarfed down a quick salad. She bit back a chuckle as she glanced at the broom standing in her kitchen. She couldn't imagine carrying that around if she had a date. Hopefully, if anything went further with Jett, she wouldn't need to go to those extremes.

She stepped through the French doors onto her balcony. The view overlooked the parking lot and, beyond it, the rolling Smoky Mountains. She'd considered buying a small house, but she wasn't ready for that kind of commitment. Not yet. The apartment gave her a low-maintenance life with a fitness room, a heated pool for year-round enjoyment, and a nature trail she still hadn't tried.

Caylee settled into her balcony chair, waiting for the delivery van. A low, throaty rumble drew her attention as a motorcycle pulled in. The bike looked familiar, scratched in the same places as the one that had wrecked right in front of her months ago. The helmeted rider swung a leg off and headed straight for her building.

Slipping indoors, Caylee peeked through the gap from behind the drapes.

The man tugged off the helmet, showing his dark hair and handsome face. Caylee's breath caught.

The scruffy wreck survivor was the same polished, charming AC hero, and he was walking up the stairs of her apartment.

Caylee bolted to her door and pressed her eye to the peephole.

Jett's footsteps echoed closer. Stopping at apartment 205, two doors down and opposite hers, he unlocked the door and stepped in.

Caylee put a hand over her mouth to muffle a giddy laugh.

He was her neighbor.

Grinning, she slid down to sit on the floor. Jett lived in her apartment complex. Right here. Close enough that she might bump into him getting the mail, or taking out her trash, or running on that mountain trail she'd been meaning to try.

What was she thinking? She shouldn't use the broom for self-defense but to bop some sense back into her brain.

She needed to be level-headed and remember to be calm and pray before she fell for a guy she barely knew—no matter how handsome he was.

Chapter 7

Jett showered, changed into shorts and a t-shirt, then stood in front of his open refrigerator and stared at the sparse contents.

The shelves contained a carton of milk about to pass the expiration date, ketchup and mustard, leftover pizza, limp cheese slices, lunch meat that had curled on the edges, and a loaf of bread sprouting green mold.

Suppressing a gag, he shut the fridge and opened his cabinets. Cereal, instant oatmeal, toaster pastries, a box of crackers, tuna, and potato chips were his choices. He definitely needed to be better about shopping for healthy food.

Jett grabbed a box of breakfast cereal, dumped some into a plastic bowl, and splashed in just enough milk to wet the flakes. He plopped onto his couch, cranked on the TV, and scrolled through channels.

The news blared with crisis after crisis, never broadcasting good news other than the usual two-second spot at the end before they wished their viewers a good day. How could anyone enjoy their day after watching the news?

Jett blew out a disgusted breath. The networks needed to carry feel-good, real-life stories like what happened with the hoarder he'd met. After Jett informed Ben regarding the man's circumstances, a group of compassionate townspeople came to help the man clean his house. In addition, they provided support to address any underlying concerns related to his compulsive behavior.

The world was filled with good people, but they seldom got the recognition that those who did wrong received.

Jett finally landed on a channel that showed how things were made. At least he wouldn't have to worry about drama, political crud, and nauseating news reports.

Once he finished eating, he'd ride his motorcycle on one of the scenic roads, swim laps in the pool, stop by the fitness room and get a workout, or run the trail — anything to get away from the world's craziness.

A ka-thunk, ka-thunk came from the stairwell, followed by a grunt that sounded like someone in a wrestling match. Jett paused mid-chew, set his bowl down, and peered through his door's peephole.

A guy who looked like he was still in high school was struggling to haul a washer up the stairway using a wobbly dolly.

Jett stepped out. "Can I give you a hand?"

"I got it," the teen said. The sweaty forehead and the way his legs trembled disputed his statement.

The washer lurched. Jett rushed over and grabbed the edge to keep it from wobbling. "Keep going. I'll keep it stable."

"Thanks, man."

"Coming through." The words boomed across the stairwell moments before a massive, muscular black man appeared, a dryer strapped across his broad back. Each step he took made the stairs creak beneath his weight. As he passed, he nodded at Jett, his eyes friendly but focused.

The man knocked on apartment 202. Without a word, he disappeared inside.

Awestruck by the man's presence, Jett turned toward the teenager. "Who was that?"

"The owner of the company. Mr. Torrence. He used to play for the NFL before he retired and opened the appliance store."

Jett had to force his mouth closed. "That was Jalen Torrence? I loved watching him play!" Seeing his childhood hero was unbelievable. Jalen wasn't just a talented player; he was known for his kindness and generosity both on the field and off.

Caylee was surprised that the owner of the company was helping with the delivery. She'd already gushed over Mr. Torrence in the store when she picked out the machines, and now she was trying not to turn into a total fan-girl.

Jalen Torrence was a football legend. Most of her girlfriends didn't understand why she enjoyed the game. Beyond the bone-shattering violence involving massive players, the catches and runs could be incredibly graceful.

Caylee stayed out of the way while he hooked up the dryer. No more carrying her laundry to and from her parents' home. Even though she enjoyed visiting with them, it would be great to be more independent again.

Her apartment door opened again, and two guys wrestled the washer inside. When they got it situated, a teen wiped his forehead and turned to his partner. "Thanks for the help, man."

"Glad to have helped."

Caylee froze. The other man was Jett! Her AC hero was in her apartment in shorts and a t-shirt, his hair still a little damp like he'd just changed after work.

Jalen clapped the teen on the shoulder. "Good work today, kid. One step at a time."

The teen straightened and smiled, then left.

Jalen turned to Jett. "Thanks for helping with the washer."

"My pleasure. Mr. Torrence, may I shake your hand? I'm a huge fan of yours."

"You bet."

Caylee waited until they finished the handshake, then stepped closer. "Jett?"

"Caylee?" His face lit up. "Small world. I didn't know you lived here."

Jalen straightened and chuckled at their reunion. "You two know each other?"

"We met where she works. I'm an HVAC tech." Jett's smiling gaze stayed on Caylee.

"A noble profession," Jalen said. "And one that is *very* appreciated when those units go on the fritz."

Caylee grinned at her AC hero. "Jett saved our department from hypothermia."

"True, but the penguins are still upset."

She snorted a laugh. *Oh no.* She didn't just do that. Heat ignited her face at her very unladylike snort.

Jett's eyes lit with humor, then he turned back to Jalen. "It's a real pleasure meeting you. You've been an inspiration to me not only in how you played but also in how you treat others off the field."

"I appreciate that." Jalen turned on the dryer and then the washer and let them run. "While we wait to make sure your machines are working properly, and since you both like football, do you mind if I share something the game taught me?"

"Not at all," Caylee and Jett said in unison.

Jalen leaned against the doorframe. "On the field, when your team has the ball, you don't just stand still. You've got to move it forward. You run, pass, whatever it takes. The clock doesn't stop for long, so you can't spend time celebrating a big gain or crying over a fumble. Last season's championship or last week's loss doesn't matter. What matters is the play right in front of you."

"Sometimes the play can't happen because of injury," Jett murmured.

Jalen nodded. "I understand. After football, I could've sat around missing the glory days or kicking myself for injuries that ended my career early. But if I did that, I'd miss what's happening right now, like building my business, or helping a customer get settled in a new place." His smile rested on Caylee for a moment. "Plus, if I didn't keep moving forward, I'd miss seeing God open doors I never expected."

Jalen's words settled in Caylee's heart. The past year, she'd been stuck far too often replaying her bad plays.

"I get that," Jett murmured. "With mistakes, some days it's easier to pull away from the world."

"Exactly, but that's not the answer." Jalen turned off the dryer and the washer, then turned back toward them. "The Bible talks about running the race set before us and keeping our eyes on the prize. And the best part, Jesus promises that He'll never leave or forsake us. You're never out there alone. So keep moving forward, one play and one day at a time."

Caylee's eyes stung a little, but in the best way. "Thank you, Mr. Torrence. I really needed to hear that."

"Call me Jalen." He gently shook her hand, then gave Jett another hearty handshake.

"Keep pressing on," the man said. "Both of you. The prize at the end is worth every step."

Caylee thanked Jalen again as she let him out of the apartment. She needed to stop looking back and start looking forward to whatever God had next for her journey.

Chapter 8

Jett stayed standing in Caylee's apartment, the words Jalen spoke lingering in his mind. He'd spent years replaying his glory days and being angry at the loss of his mom and his soccer career, never watching to see what God might have planned next.

"Thank you for helping the deliverymen." Caylee stepped beside him. "I hope you didn't mind the sermon." A flicker of embarrassment crossed her face.

"Are you kidding? Getting to meet Jalen and listen to what he shared was incredible. That wasn't a sermon. That was a life lesson. And something I needed to hear."

Caylee's face softened, the relief in her eyes tugging at him. She nodded. "Yeah, I did too."

Jett wanted to say something, but the silence seemed fitting, as if both of them needed a quiet moment. He hadn't realized how much he'd been craving a conversation with someone other than Ben and his family, or work clients.

He wasn't ready to leave Caylee. "Want to walk on the trail with me? We've still got daylight for a little while."

Her blue-eyed gaze met his. "I'd like that."

The path from the apartment complex wound up a small hill and back down again. The late evening light filtered through the canopy of the trees as they reached a small stream.

Sitting together on a large rock at the water's edge, they dangled their legs above the current.

Caylee's shoulder brushed his. Her warmth seeping through his sleeve reminded him how long it had been since he'd let anyone get this close.

After his soccer career ended, he kept busy trying to avoid life by going in early and working late or traveling around the country.

Jett drew in a breath and stared at the sky above. "You know, after Jalen's talk about moving forward, it feels like God might be trying to get through to me."

Caylee turned toward him. "Like what?"

Her steady, encouraging gaze made the words come easier, loosening something tight inside his chest. "Maybe I've been stuck hiding, not really playing."

"I get what you mean," she whispered. "I've spent months beating myself up over an unhealthy relationship. Hearing Jalen say we're never alone reminded me I need to trust God and stop replaying the old regrets."

Jett nodded. Considered taking her hand in his, but he hesitated, afraid to break the moment between them.

A bird's faint chirps blended with the chorus of cricket songs.

"Did you play football?" Caylee asked.

"No. Soccer."

"I'm surprised. I thought the way you gushed over Jalen that you played the game."

"No, my dad preferred soccer." From as early as he could remember, soccer was simply what he did and who he was. Was the game his passion, or what his dad had wanted?

"Did you play in high school and college?" Caylee asked.

It took a minute for Jett to refocus his thoughts. "Both until I couldn't."

"What happened?"

Jett's jaw clenched. He forced it to relax. "A bad hit stopped my heart."

Caylee sucked in a breath. "Oh, my goodness! Are you okay?"

"I'm alive, but it stopped my career." He forced a smile.

She laid her hand on his arm. "I'm sorry," she whispered. Her brow creased, and a flicker of concern crossed her face as her grip tightened on his arm. "Wait. You ride a motorcycle and mess with live wires that could shock you into kingdom come, and *that's* safer than soccer?"

Jett wasn't sure whether to laugh or cringe. "Can't play it safe all the time." Not that the doctors or his coaches had given him a choice. He needed a subject change. "How about you? Did you play sports?"

"No," Caylee withdrew her hand, tucking it against her side. "I'm too short and too uncoordinated for sports or cheerleading."

Jett shot her a curious look, a small grin tugging at his lips. "So, you went into accounting?"

"Life doesn't always add up, but numbers do." Her smile stopped short of her eyes. Then her gaze drifted toward the nearby trees.

After a moment, Caylee's posture straightened, and she smiled. "I'm sure you were great at soccer, but I'm grateful you chose the job you did. How else would I have been saved from freezing to death or being attacked by penguins?"

He grinned at the beautiful woman next to him. Maybe his life being rerouted off the soccer field was for something better than he could have imagined.

A gurgling sound drew his attention to the water. Caught in the stream's pull, a tangle of leaves clung stubbornly to the stones. Jett reached for a fallen branch and prodded the cluster until it broke loose.

The leaves spun away, swirling free into the current. Jett sat back, hands braced on the warm rock, watching the water flow unhindered. The old roar of the stadium crowd flickered once in his mind, then dimmed, giving way to something quieter. Something new.

He glanced at Caylee. "Life's funny. First, I crash into your world on my bike. Then I show up at your office to fix the AC. Next thing, I'm hauling a washer into your place."

"I'm grateful God dropped you into my playing field." A hint of mischief sparked in her eyes. "Not many people have the power to change the weather."

"I am a man of many talents." Jett puffed out his chest. "Weather controller and penguin wrangler extraordinaire at your service."

Caylee grinned. "Thanks for tonight."

"The pleasure is all mine." Jett paused for a moment. "It feels good to be moving again."

"Yeah, it does. I'm glad we're figuring this out together."

Jett saluted. "Team Ryder at your service."

"Your last name's Ryder? Like, Jett Rider?"

"Ryder spelled with a y, not an i, and I've heard every joke in the book."

"I think it's a cool name."

Her sweet smile sent a flush of heat creeping up the back of his neck. "Thanks." Jett glanced up at the darkening sky. He stood and offered her a hand. "I'd better get you home."

Her soft fingers lingered in his as she rose. For a moment, they stood close, her blue eyes searching his.

Jett's gaze dropped to her lips. Caylee's breath caught, and he imagined closing the distance. The temptation was right there, but he didn't want to risk spoiling the moment, or the fragile start of whatever this might become. "I'll race you back," he said instead.

Surprise lit her face for a moment, then her eyes playfully narrowed. "You're on."

Leaves crunched underfoot as she sprinted ahead, her laughter trailing behind.

With a chuckle, Jett gave chase.

Caylee slowed at the base of the stairs, her heart still racing. "Okay, note to self." She pressed a hand to her side. "Power-walking in the dark is not for the faint of heart."

Jett chuckled. "I thought we were training for the next Olympic speed-hiking event."

"Hey, I was keeping up with the guy who runs trails for fun." She bumped his arm. "Admit it. You were showing off."

"Guilty as charged."

Not in a rush to end the evening, Caylee slowly climbed the stairs. As she went to unlock her door, her keys slipped and clattered to the floor. Before she could bend down, Jett scooped them up, handing them back with a small bow.

"Your door awaits, my lady."

Caylee's fingers brushed his as she took the keys. "Thanks, Sir Galahad of the AC world."

Jett leaned against the wall beside her door, crossing his arms. "How about we do this again? After work tomorrow, if you're feeling adventurous, I could show you my favorite spot further up the trail."

"You've got a deal." Caylee unlocked her door and turned toward him.

He stepped back. "Goodnight, Caylee."

"Goodnight." Smiling, she slipped inside.

Caylee got a glass of water and stared at the broom. "Not tonight, my bristled friend. Your services are not needed."

Chapter 9

"**M**ost boring meeting ever,"

Caylee grinned at Amy's dramatic comment as they walked back to their department. "It wasn't that bad."

"Yes, it was." Amy opened the door into their area and paused, waiting until Caylee went in. "An entire hour of sitting while some guy droned on and on about something they could have sent in an email."

"Would you have read it?" Caylee settled into her office chair.

"Probably not." Amy propped her backside on the desk.

"How else would we have heard the leadership updates, company wins, and the best part, financials?"

"Okay," Amy rolled her eyes. "I did like hearing about the company's new tech stuff."

"See, it was a good meeting," Caylee moved her mouse to wake up her computer. The screen flickered to life.

"Fine, but it took me away from what I really wanted to be doing."

"Work?"

"No," Amy leaned toward her. "I want to know why you've been smiling all morning."

Caylee could hardly hold in her excitement. "Guess who lives in our apartment complex?"

"From the look on your face, it must be someone wonderful. Is it the hunkiest man alive?"

"No, but close," Caylee sighed. "Our AC hero."

"Oh, yeah, baby." Amy playfully wagged her eyebrows. "He is a hunk. Which building does he live in?"

"He's in mine, and he's all mine."

"Possessive already? What's been going on?"

Caylee smiled at the memory of hanging out with Jett. "We went for a walk last evening, sat by a stream, and talked."

"No huggy and kissy?"

"No, Jett was a perfect gentleman." Not that she wouldn't mind a little kissing and hugging. "He's going to show me his favorite spot up the trail from where we went last night."

"Mmmm, sounds interesting." Amy did a dramatic swoon against the cubicle wall. "So if he shows up tonight with a picnic and a guitar, are we calling this a date or still just friends?"

"Oh, please. It's not a big deal." Of course, Caylee wouldn't mind if the relationship grew into something more than friendship.

"So, let me get this straight. You're infatuated with someone you barely know. And yet, you kept telling me that after your last boyfriend, you wanted nothing to do with men."

Caylee shifted in her seat, fingers toying with the edge of a paperclip. "Well, that was before Jett."

"Don't get me wrong. I'm happy for you, but you made me promise I wouldn't let you jump into another relationship without the guy being thoroughly checked out."

"Ugh. You're right. But Jett seems different."

"You said that's why you liked Winfred, Winkleman, or whatever his name was."

"Winthrop." Caylee flinched at the name. She had gotten all excited about Jett just like she had at first with Winthrop. But surely the men were nothing alike.

Winthrop had been more interested in showing off, showing out, and trying to get physical with her. And she'd spent years in a relationship she knew wasn't good. She inwardly groaned, pressing her fingers to her forehead as if wishing she could erase the memory. Caylee glanced at her friend. "Don't you have invoices to process?"

Amy let out a dramatic sigh. "Fine." She shuffled toward the door. "I'll go back to my own cubicle and do my own work, by my all alone self."

"Go on, Ms. Dramatic." Caylee playfully swatted her friend with a folder. "And I promise, I'll be careful with Jett."

Amy paused. "One more thing. If he turns out to be another smooth-talking show-off, I'm staging an intervention. With snacks for me and a PowerPoint entitled Why Caylee Deserves Better Than Flashy Jerks."

Caylee chuckled. "Thanks, friend."

After Amy left, Caylee put her head in her hands and moaned. Was she being taken in by another handsome guy? She didn't think so, but could she trust herself? What if she fell hard and fast and got into another situation that got messy and went the wrong way?

Why on earth had she ever had anything to do with Winthrop? Had she been so starved for attention that she let herself be bought for clothes, jewelry, and a good time out on the town?

Winthrop never listened when she talked about her faith, whereas Jett actually seemed to care. Closing her eyes, Caylee sent up a prayer for help. "Lord, if Jett is not in Your perfect plan, please give me the strength to walk away before I make another terrible mistake."

Jett checked the time. Only a few more hours until he'd see Caylee again. He planned to take her to a small waterfall where they could kick off their shoes and wade into the water. And if things went well, maybe it would become the beginning of many more evenings spent together.

Jett lugged his tools up the creaky pull-down stairs and entered the customer's attic. The temperature had to be twenty degrees hotter than the sun. Sweat instantly covered his body, making his shirt stick to his back as he crossed the sketchy rafters to check the unit that had been installed in the seventies.

How it had kept running all those years in an attic without insulation was beyond him. If he hadn't been so hot, he would have saluted the old machine.

There was no way he could get parts. Hopefully, he could do something to get it to work.

Even though the ancient house and yard were immaculately kept, by the looks of the older couple's furnishings, it was obvious they were barely scraping by.

Saying a prayer for help for them and their AC unit, Jett opened a panel and stared inside.

What on earth?

Leaves, pine needles, and other material were stuffed inside. Not sure if it was a rat's nest or some other nasty rodent, Jett put on gloves and opened a garbage bag he kept with his tools.

Reaching into the unit to untangle the chaotic mess, his nose wrinkled at a strange, pungent odor, and his fingers touched something unexpectedly warm.

A squirrel exploded from the leaves, sprinted up his arm, and launched a full-scale assault on his hair.

Tiny, sharp claws scrambling across his head, Jett yelped, his arms flailing, trying to get rid of the crazy rodent.

His boot slid on the dusty beam, and he bonked his head on an overhead rafter and grabbed it for support.

The squirrel thrashed Jett's head with frenzied energy, sending flecks of dust and a stray leaf into Jett's mouth. He coughed, praying he hadn't swallowed squirrel debris.

With a final tap-dance, it leaped from Jett's head and escaped through a roof mushroom vent.

Hoping the squirrel hadn't given him an impromptu bald patch, Jett ran his fingers through his hair, half-expecting to find fur, acorns, or tiny woodland tokens.

He blew out a breath and said a prayer, thanking God that he hadn't fallen through the rafters. He added a request that any other rodent attacks be outside, where he had a better fighting chance.

Jett leaned over, trying to catch his breath. The heat caused sweat to trickle down his back, collecting in his pants and giving the impression of a more strenuous event than a mere squirrel skirmish.

Once his composure somewhat returned, he glanced up at the vent where the squirrel had exited. He needed to seal that opening. Checking through his toolkit, he found wire mesh. His dad had trained him to be ready for anything, so his toolkit held a variety of materials for whatever he might encounter.

With a hammer, nails, and a mesh patch, Jett made sure there was no way that squirrel would get back inside the attic, at least from that location.

That task completed, he finished cleaning and checking the unit for any damaged wires or loose connections.

The sound of scratching overhead drew his attention. Squirrel monster was back and even angrier, chewing and scratching at the vent like he or she wanted to get back in and tear Jett's head off.

He hurried to get the rest of the nest safely inside the bag, then rushed down the attic stairs and ran to the backyard.

"Hey, squirrel," he yelled to the roof.

The rodent scurried toward the edge, and Jett was sure the squirrel's eyes narrowed as it stared at him.

"I've got your nest." Jett opened the bag and set it securely between two branches of a nearby tree. Backing up, he waited.

The squirrel, tail-flicking, remained motionless for a moment, then sprang onto the tree and gingerly sniffed the nest. The furry-fiend gave another look that Jett hoped was one of approval.

He gave a nod. "You're welcome."

Back in the attic, Jett turned on the machine and couldn't believe his ears. The unit started up and purred like a new one. Guess the old fella just needed to be cleaned out.

He patted the AC unit, then sealed that opening so nothing could get inside. He said another silent thanks to God for helping him against ninja rodents and getting the machine running again.

Jett rubbed his hand through his hair again, as though it might still be crawling with tiny squirrel invaders. His dad had always told him they were just rats with good PR.

Thank goodness, the office had showers, paid for cleaning employees' uniforms, and Jett kept a fresh change of clothes in his locker. As soon as he got there, he'd rinse his mouth out a thousand times and take a shower with every soap product available.

Picking up his toolkit, Jett swung it over his shoulder. Lord willing, the evening with Caylee would be much, much better.

"I will never, ever have a pet squirrel. No feeders, no nut bowls. Nothing," Jett muttered as he went down the attic stairs.

Chapter 10

Standing with Jett on the trail, Caylee gasped for air, her sides burning from laughter as he hilariously reenacted the squirrel attack.

She leaned against the tree to catch her breath. Still giggling, she pointed at Jett's head. "You do seem to have a little bald spot."

He frantically patted his scalp. "Seriously? I'm missing a chunk?"

"I'm just messing with you." She nodded toward a squirrel perched on a branch overhead, tail flicking like it was plotting revenge. "But I'd watch your back."

Jett's eyes narrowed as he scanned the trees. "Is it just me, or is there an abundance of furry rodents out this evening?"

"Be brave, my squirrel whisperer." Caylee casually bumped him as they kept walking, her elbow lingering a second against his side.

The trail narrowed until their shoulders brushed with every few steps, her skin tingling with each accidental touch.

Caylee reminded herself it was just a hike. Nothing more. She needed to remember Winthrop's charming smiles, easy promises, and then he was gone when it mattered. She pushed the memory away, focusing on the light filtering through the oak and hickory leaves.

"You've heard about my day," Jett said. "How was yours?"

"Nothing special. Invoices, spreadsheets, and data." She drew in a deep breath of the fresh air. "It's nice to get outside."

Jett nodded. "Yeah, that's one good thing about my job. I'm not cramped in an office." He glanced her way. "Not that there's anything wrong with that."

"I get what you're saying. I love my job, but it would be nice to have a sunroof over my desk."

Like a streak of gray lightning, a squirrel raced across the path ahead of them.

Jett threw out his arm like a hero in an action movie. "Save yourself!"

Laughing, Caylee ducked under his arm and popped up beside him. "My hero. Did you just try to shield me from a squirrel?"

Jett lowered his arm but didn't step away from her. "It was moving fast. Could've been rabid. Or a ninja rodent. You never know."

"Thank you for saving me. We'd better get out of the danger zone before a squirrel army shows up."

Jett glanced her way, a half-smile tugging at his lips. "So you'd put a sunroof over your desk?"

"Yes, I would. I'd have a hammock where I could just float above my desk and pretend I'm on a beach somewhere."

They kept walking as the trail gently climbed. The trees thinned, opening up to a breathtaking panorama of rolling Tennessee hills, their blue ridges fading into the distance under the late-afternoon sky.

"It's gorgeous," Caylee breathed.

"Definitely," Jett wasn't looking at the view. His gaze was steady on her.

Her cheeks burning, she looked away. She needed to slow down. She barely knew him.

"Come on." Jett motioned with his chin. "I'll show you the waterfall."

He led her down a side trail that dipped to the left. The path narrowed, leading to a stream where a small waterfall tumbled over slick, mossy stones.

Jett motioned with his chin. "I like to sit on that big rock in the middle. It's my place to come after tough days." He held out his hand. "Want to wade in and sit with me for a while?"

Caylee hesitated only a second.

They kicked off their shoes and left them on the shore. He took her hand, steadying her as they stepped into the clear stream.

She sucked in a breath at the cold rush around her ankles. "That's colder than I thought it would be."

Jett grinned. "It's nice, isn't it?"

Hand in hand, they waded the rest of the way. Sitting side by side on the flat rock, they dangled their feet in the current.

"The first week I moved to Garden Valley, I found this place," Jett said quietly. "Watching the water flow around the rocks is soothing. Helps me pray through the hard stuff."

Caylee nodded, staring at the sparkling water. "It is nice. In Florida, most of our rivers and streams aren't clear like this."

"Do you miss the beach?"

"I liked the ocean breeze, but I wasn't much of a hang-out-in-the-sand type of girl." She shrugged, the old loneliness creeping in. Not that anyone had ever asked her to join them for beach parties.

"Too much grit in places that shouldn't get gritty?"

"That was part of it." She paused a moment, then grinned at him." The Tennessee hills are becoming my favorite place."

His gaze swept across her face. "They're becoming mine too."

As much as she would love to gaze into Jett's eyes for a thousand years, Caylee pretended to stare at the trees for a moment. "How about you? Do you miss where you grew up?"

"Not really. Mom passed eleven years ago. Dad remarried and moved to Vegas."

Caylee gripped the rock's edge. "I'm so sorry."

Jett shrugged. "No big deal." But the tightness around his eyes said otherwise.

Caylee thought of her own family and how it would hurt to lose them. No matter how old she got, she still wanted that family connection.

A bird trilled from a nearby tree, its song answered by another in the distance.

Jett cleared his throat. "Okay, so funny AC story."

It took her a second to shift gears.

"A panicked guy called," Jett continued, "saying his house was stifling hot when they returned from vacation. I got there and found the breaker flipped off. Turns out the man had turned it off to save on the electric bill while they were gone. His wife and kids looked at me like I had saved their lives."

Caylee giggled. "Must be nice to be the hero."

Jett turned toward her. "What's the funniest thing that's happened in accounting?"

"During college, while working the year-end close at my company, a new intern mistakenly processed every single vendor payment twice. Thankfully, my supervisor caught it before they went out. The intern was mortified and kept saying he was only trying to be thorough."

"Thorough is one word for it."

Caylee grinned at the man beside her. He seemed so thoughtful, so handsome, so sweet. Goodness, she was falling fast and hard.

Part of her wanted to let this feeling sweep her away, while the other part whispered caution. She needed to remember how Winthrop made her feel special until he didn't.

"I'd better get you home." Jett stood, offering his hand again.

Caylee took it, and they started back through the stream.

Her foot slipped on a moss-covered rock, and she stumbled backward.

Jett caught her, pulling her close against his chest. "You okay?"

For a moment, neither moved. His strong and fast heartbeat thumped against hers.

Her hands gripping his shoulders, Caylee nodded. "Yeah. Thanks for the save."

"Anytime." Jett's gaze drifted to her lips.

Caylee whimpered. Jett had to be the sweetest man she'd ever known, and kissing him would be incredibly enjoyable.

Before she could stop herself, she leaned in and pressed her lips to his.

He froze for half a second, then returned the kiss, soft at first, then more urgent, as her fingers threaded into his hair.

What was she thinking?

Caylee pushed away, stumbling to the shore. "I'm so sorry! I shouldn't have done that. Oh my goodness, why did I do that?" She yanked on her shoes, then ran down the trail.

Jett's voice trailed behind her. "Caylee!"

Tears blurred the trail ahead. *Not again. Not with someone good.* Winthrop had been a jerk, and she'd known it, but she'd repeatedly gone back to him.

She could *not* trust herself.

Jett caught up. "Hey, I'm sorry I got out of control."

She stopped, breathing hard, tears pooling in her eyes. "You? It wasn't you. It was me."

He stepped closer but kept a distance. "It was a great kiss."

"Yes, it was." Too great. She turned away. "I'm so sorry. I'm trying to be good."

Jett chuckled.

Caylee pivoted to face him. "Don't make fun of me."

"I'm not. I'm sorry. I'm the one having a tough time behaving." He shoved his hands into his pockets. "Caylee, you're gorgeous and fun to be with. I don't want to mess up our friendship, or whatever this is. I'll keep my hands to myself from now on."

Caylee whimpered. "But that's not what I want." Oh, good grief, she was a pitiful mess.

"You don't?"

She stared at her shoes. "You're great, and I really enjoy being with you, and you're a wonderful kisser."

Jett took her hand in his. "Caylee, you have nothing to apologize for. Kissing isn't a sin."

She didn't want to explain why she was so upset. "But first you're attacked by a squirrel, then assaulted by me."

He smiled. "I much prefer your kind of attack."

"Well, at least I didn't leave a nest you had to clean up."

Jett chuckled. "How about we try something different? Be a little more cautious. If you like Mexican food, we could go to Rosie's. My treat."

Caylee squeezed his fingers. "I'd like that."

Jett walked her to her door, gave her a brief hug, then stepped back. "Thanks for a great evening." He took her hand in his. "We're okay, Caylee. Really."

She said goodnight and closed her apartment door. Touching her lips, she replayed the kiss. What was wrong with her?

She forced her hand to her side. She'd thrown caution out the window again.

A knock echoed from across the hall, and Caylee peeked through her peephole.

An attractive woman holding a canvas bag stood at Jett's apartment. As he opened the door, the woman laughed at something he said as she went inside. The door clicked shut behind them.

Caylee leaned her forehead against the wood. Of course. She should have known better than to trust a man so soon.

Her phone buzzed.

Jett's text: *Thanks again for the really great evening. Sleep well.*

Caylee stared at the message. With a groan, she tossed her phone aside.

She slid to the floor, hugging her knees. "Lord, why is it so hard for me to trust myself, trust men, and to trust You with my heart?"

Back in his apartment, Jett set the bag of leftovers in the fridge. Evidently, his cousin had been worried enough about Jett's poor eating habits to send his wife, Tiffany, over with food.

Jett opened the French doors leading to his balcony and stepped outside. Holding Caylee close, her hands gripping his shoulders, he'd felt old instincts flare, the old habits of charming his way through flings without commitment.

But that wasn't him anymore.

He'd spent too many days and nights asking God to make him better, someone who valued the woman in front of him more than the moment.

Caylee wasn't just fun. She was someone he wanted to have a chance with long-term.

Jett glanced at the stars blinking in the night sky and prayed that God would help him be a man worthy of a godly relationship.

He didn't want to be who he was before.

Chapter 11

The next morning, Caylee sat at her desk, staring at the same spreadsheet she'd opened twenty minutes earlier. The numbers blurred into a meaningless sea of black and white. The low thrum of office chatter sounded distant, muffled, as if she were underwater.

All she could see was Jett's smiling face, the way his clean scent lingered in her memory, the comforting heat of his chest against her, and his surprised smile right before their kiss.

Then she'd seen the woman at his door, laughing, then breezing inside his apartment.

Caylee pressed her palms against her eyes to hold back her tears.

A knock on her cubicle wall jolted her back to the present. Caylee straightened.

Amy leaned in, holding two steaming coffees from the cafeteria. "You look like you got hit by a truck." She slid one cup toward Caylee and perched on the edge of the desk. "Spill. What happened last night? I thought you had gone out with Jett."

"I did." Caylee swiped at her eyes and kept her voice low. "We kissed."

"You kissed our superhero AC guy?" Amy swayed dramatically, fanning herself with a flourish.

Caylee's cheeks flushed hot with embarrassment. "I slipped in a stream, and Jett caught me, and I leaned in like a love-sick teenager and kissed him. *Really* kissed him. And then I panicked and ran."

Amy stared for a beat, then burst out laughing. "You kissed him, then bolted?"

"Pretty much." Caylee groaned. "I kept apologizing to God the entire way back. Jett was sweet about it and even asked me to dinner at Rosie's. His treat."

"I'm sure Jett didn't mind the kiss at all. So why were you apologizing to God and looking so miserable?"

"Because I shouldn't have kissed Jett. We barely know one another. And I don't want to screw up again." Caylee stared into her dark coffee. "And then right after Jett dropped me off, I saw an attractive woman at his apartment. Holding a bag. He let her in, and she laughed like they were old friends. Or more."

Amy's teasing grin faded. "Ouch."

"Yeah. Ouch. I stood there peeking through my peephole, feeling that sick, stomach-dropping feeling like I did with Winthrop."

"Hey," Amy reached over and squeezed Caylee's arm. "From what you've described, Winthrop was a jerk. Jett's probably nothing like him. You said he's thoughtful and sweet."

"Yeah, but what if I'm falling for a guy I shouldn't? I prayed last night and asked God why it's so hard to trust myself or Him with my heart. I don't know if I'm making a mistake or if God's given me a gift. And then I ignored Jett's goodnight text."

Amy was quiet for a moment. "Okay. First, being cautious is good. That's not weakness, that's wisdom. Second, give Jett the benefit of the doubt. One woman with a bag doesn't mean he's hiding a secret girlfriend. She could be a friend or a family member. You don't know yet."

Caylee took a shaky breath. "Maybe you're right."

"Look, you don't have to decide everything today. Go to Rosie's. Eat tacos or fajitas or drown yourself in spicy salsa. See how Jett acts. If he's dodging questions or acting shady, you walk. Trust doesn't mean zero caution; it means taking one careful step at a time."

"Yeah," Caylee nodded, the tension in her shoulders easing. "I'm overthinking. I shouldn't think the worst about Jett."

"Text him back. Say yes to tonight." Amy stood. "And then let me know what happens. Deal?"

"Deal." Caylee picked up her phone, found Jett's text, and sent a quick reply.

Still on for Rosie's? I'm game if you are.

Finished early with his calls, Jett parked his van at the office, checked his phone, and grinned at Caylee's text. Good thing he'd been where he could reply.

He'd worried last night and this morning when he hadn't heard from her. He sent a response that he'd pick her up at six, hoping this was moving the relationship forward another step.

Having dinner together would be great. Then again, would Caylee want to ride on the back of his motorcycle? Nothing says romance like showing up windblown, soaked from rain, or frozen from sleet.

Time to adult and trade the bike in for a car. His credit was good, and he had enough money in savings for a down payment.

Jett entered the building and walked to get a shower and change.

"Everything okay?" Ben kept in step with Jett as they made their way through the building. "You seemed distracted when you left early this morning."

"I'm good now. Going out tonight with Caylee."

"Sounds like things are moving forward."

"I hope so," Jett said. "Caylee's special. And thanks again for the leftovers. Tiffany's cooking is saving my life."

Ben chuckled as he held the door open to the employee area. "Yeah, Tiff was worried you weren't eating well. Said you looked like you needed home-cooked food."

"She's right. Tell her thanks. And not to worry, tonight I'm taking Caylee for Mexican food." Jett put his tools in his locker and turned to his cousin. "Hey, do you know anyone who might have a decent car for sale?"

"You thinking of selling your motorcycle?"

"Yeah, it's time. Rainy days are the pits, and I don't want to go through another winter on the bike." Jett shuddered just thinking about driving hilly, icy roads and the bone-deep chill that never seemed to leave.

"As a matter of fact," Ben said. "I know someone who would be thrilled to make you a good deal."

"Great." Jett grinned at the thought of taking another step from the past. "Do you have their number?"

"I have a better idea. If you're through with your calls for the day, follow me to my father-in-law's place."

"He's selling a car?"

"It's not just any vehicle; it's a cherry red 2004 Ford Mustang GT, 4.6 liter with a 260 horsepower V8."

Jett whistled as he hung his tools in his locker. "Man, that sounds great. Why is he giving it up?"

"My mother-in-law put her foot down and told him he needed to grow up and be a proper granddad. The car's been Silas's baby for years. He doesn't have it listed yet, so if you promise to treat her right, he'll probably give you a good deal."

"That would be amazing."

"Silas would want to meet you and make sure you're the type who'll keep his baby running well. I even know a guy who might want to buy your motorcycle. I'll call Silas and see if he's available to meet with us."

"Great. I'll get ready and meet you in the lobby." Jett sent a silent prayer up for favor if God was okay with him buying the Mustang. The motorcycle had been a rebellious poke at his dad, who hated them. It was time to grow up.

Jett showered and changed, then used his phone to check online to see how much a car like that would cost. The price range listed would be doable on his salary, especially if he sold his motorcycle for a decent amount.

Between his apartment rent and other expenses, he'd still have enough to keep his savings account growing. The more time he spent in Garden Valley, the more he wanted to stay.

Jett glanced again at Caylee's text. Her laugh, humor, honesty, and faith made him want to be better and do better.

Lord willing, by staying, he was finally heading in the right direction.

Chapter 12

Jett circled the Mustang one more time. The car sat in an immaculate garage with tools lined up on the pegboard walls. Fluorescent lights highlighted the car's deep red paint.

Silas Stafford stood watching, tall and lean, easily six-three with salt-and-pepper hair. "You know engines?" Silas asked, voice low and gravelly.

"Yeah," Jett cleared his throat. "I mean, yes, sir. My dad had me working on the company trucks since I was old enough to hold a socket." The memory struck him, leaving him disoriented for a moment. His dad wasn't big on hugs or words, especially after Jett's mom died. Was learning HVAC and working on vehicles together, how his dad showed he cared?

Silas popped the hood; the sound brought Jett back to the present. "She's got miles. Windows stick when it rains, same as my knees. Spark plugs need watching. I'm not chasing top dollar. I want someone who'll treat her right."

"I'd be honored, sir. I'd keep her safe and pampered."

Silas's eyes narrowed. "Got a garage?"

Jett winced. "Apartment. But I'd get a good breathable cover, the kind that doesn't trap moisture. Tuck the car in every night. I'm saving for a house with a garage."

The man's jaw worked like he was chewing the words over. "Ben told me you were a good guy. Hard worker. Thought of well by customers. You planning to stay?"

"Yes, sir. I'm ready to settle."

After a long beat, Silas tossed the keys at Jett. "Get in. Show me how you drive."

Jett slid behind the wheel. The V8's engine rumbled to life, vibrating through the leather seats. He drove like he was hauling fragile cargo, making full stops at every sign, smooth turns, and nothing jerky.

Arms crossed, Silas watched like he was measuring Jett's every move.

Back in the garage, Jett turned off the engine and handed Silas back the keys.

The man leaned against the workbench, his face a storm of emotions.

Waiting, sweat traced a slow path down Jett's spine.

Ben leaned close. "Asking for Tiffany's hand was worse. I aged a decade that day."

Silas huffed a breath, then named a price so low Jett nearly laughed.

He straightened, looking serious. "I'll hit the bank first thing for financing—"

"No," Silas cut him off. "I'll carry the note. Fair rate. You make payments, you keep her shining."

Jett's throat tightened. "Really? I don't even know what to say. Thank you."

Silas's gaze flicked outside to the motorcycle parked in the driveway. "That yours?"

"Yes, sir. Took a slide when an animal jumped out. The bike still runs great, though."

Silas circled the motorcycle, his hand trailing the scratches and marred paint. "God's creatures deserve saving. So do the people on the road. And the machines we trust with our lives."

Jett rubbed the back of his neck. "I wasn't speeding, sir."

Muttering, Silas pulled out his phone and scrolled through web pages. Then he grabbed Ben's elbow and drew him aside. Their hushed voices carried glances Jett's way.

Jett stared at the Mustang. Maybe the car wasn't meant for him. Not after the drifting and the years spent running from everything that mattered. God probably wanted him in something boring and plain to keep him humble.

Silas walked back to where Jett stood waiting. "One thing I learned too late in life, son. Our things, cars, houses, money, should never outrank the people God puts in our path."

Jett nodded. "Yes, sir."

"I'll take the motorcycle as partial payment for the Mustang," Silas thumbed toward the bike. "Sell her to a buddy who'll fix her up proper."

Jett's mouth opened, closed. "You're serious?"

"Dead serious. Do right by the car and keep doing right in your life."

Astonished and thankful, Jett extended his hand. "Yes, sir."

Silas gave a hard shake. "I'm counting on you."

As Silas stepped inside for the papers, Ben clapped Jett's shoulder. "New chapter, brother."

Jett stared at the car that was soon to be his. "I never thought buying a car would be this easy and feel like forgiveness." He'd traveled too many roads and made too many wrong turns. Thankfully, the miles had led him to Garden Valley.

Silas returned, and after they signed the papers, he pressed the keys into Jett's hand. "Bring her back for visits. I'll show you how to keep that rumble just right. Garage is always open."

"I promise, sir. Oil changes, checkups, whatever she needs."

"We're family now, boy. Take good care of our girl," Silas pulled Jett into a sudden bear hug. He froze at first, then let himself lean into the embrace.

Family. Jett blinked hard to hide the sting in his eyes. He managed a hoarse "Yes, sir. I will."

Trading the bike felt like closing the book on the lone-wolf years. The car had room for people, for more than just him.

After another round of thanks, Jett drove home under the evening sky. Pulling into the apartment lot, he killed the engine and let it tick down.

Up on the balcony, a light glowed in Caylee's place. Maybe this new chapter would be about more than a car, but finding a place to belong.

He got out of the car, took his phone, snapped a photo of the car, and sent it to his dad.

He didn't know what came next, but he was ready to find out.

Chapter 13

A Spanish love song playing softly overhead, Caylee followed the waiter through Rosie's restaurant. Jett stayed close, his hand brushing the small of her back as they weaved between tables filled with families, couples, and a few people Caylee recognized from work.

Jett pulled out a chair for her. She thanked him as she sat. He took the seat across from her, his gaze flicking around the room as if taking everything in before he smiled her way.

A waiter appeared with menus and a basket of warm chips, then took their drink orders before disappearing again.

Caylee reached for a chip and dipped it into the salsa. "I love your Mustang. Your motorcycle was nice, but the car is great."

"Thanks. I still can't believe how it all worked out."

"The Mustang suits you. Besides, I was dreading getting helmet hair from riding on the back of a motorcycle. Plus, I've seen how you take curves," she teased.

"Hey, I've never crashed before that day. The bike took a hit, but a squirrel was saved." Jett squared his shoulders and gave a playful little grin, as if trying to look extra impressive.

Caylee offered him a chip as though giving him a reward. "You're a wildlife and AC hero. Although the attic rodent missed the memo."

Jett took it from her with a cute nod. "Obviously, the squirrel news channel skipped the feel-good segment."

Laughter came from a group toward the back, as though agreeing with his fun statement.

Jett scooped salsa onto the chip. "Okay, funny work story. I got called out because a lady said her house was sweating. Not sweltering, but sweating. When I showed up, I found the thermostat set to off. She thought she was saving energy by setting it to energy-efficient mode. I had to explain that off means no AC."

"Poor woman. I bet her house really was sweating."

"It was crazy hot until I turned the unit back on. Okay, your turn. Interesting or funny work story."

A waitress passed carrying a sizzling tray of food, and Caylee tried not to lean into the smoky scent. Instead, she grabbed a chip and chewed while she thought of something to share with Jett.

"At the job I had before SAU Tech, the entire department got locked out because someone formatted the numerical entries as date columns. Every cell turned into pound signs, or what most people call hashtags, because the numbers were too big. It took hours to figure out the company hadn't gone bankrupt."

The corners of Jett's eyes crinkled with his smile. "Pesky hashtags."

The server took their order. Caylee chose chicken fajitas, and Jett chose carne asada.

At the next table, a young father sat with a little boy, who looked no older than three. The child kept trying to get his taco to his mouth, but bits of lettuce and cheese kept tumbling out.

"Here, buddy," the dad guided his son's small hands. "Hold it tight, just like this."

The little boy straightened his back. "I do it!"

The dad's kind smile never faltered. "You're doing great. Tacos are tricky, but you'll get the hang of it. I'll help if you need me."

The boy took a moment before giving a small nod, and the dad patiently helped again.

Success achieved. The little boy giggled and wiped his face with the back of his hand.

Caylee motioned toward that table. "Were you an I-can-do-it kind of kid?"

Jett's eyes lingered on the father before shifting to her. "Yeah, I probably didn't make it easy on my parents."

Their server returned, balancing a tray with their steaming dishes. As he set the sizzling fajitas in front of Caylee, the smoke enveloped her like a steamy facial.

"So, what other stories do you have to share?" Caylee held a warm tortilla and tucked the savory chicken, peppers, and onions inside. The first bite sent a burst of smoky flavor across her tongue, and a moan escaped before she could stop it.

Jett's laugh rumbled low. "Careful, you might get us kicked out for disturbing the peace."

"Blame the fajitas." Caylee pushed the cast-iron skillet toward him. "Try these. The peppers are perfect."

Jett speared one with his fork, popped it into his mouth, and gave an appreciative nod. "My Carne Asada's good, but that's next level." He leaned in a fraction. "Careful sharing bites like that, I might start thinking you're trying to win me over with food."

Caylee gave him a sassy look. "Maybe I'll cook for you sometime."

"Careful what you promise. I take invitations seriously."

The scent of sizzling fajitas mingled with laughter and the soft strum of a guitar, making the crowded room suddenly feel more private.

His knee brushed hers under the table. She didn't move away.

Jett cleared his throat. "So, any other fun work stories?"

Caylee took a big drink of her cold iced tea to cool her heated cheeks. "I used to work at a place with a coffee fund jar. One day, the jar and the money went missing. Everyone was pointing fingers until the boss checked the security camera. The office cat had knocked the jar over, batted the bills around, and everything ended up underneath a bookcase. We called it the feline audit."

"That's great. Did you make the cat the CFO, Chief Feline Officer?"

"Good one, Mr. Ryder."

"Thank you, ma'am." Jett gave a contented sigh as he rubbed his flat stomach. "Good time and good food. I don't do much cooking, so my meals aren't this appetizing. Other than when my cousin's wife drops off leftovers. Kind of embarrassing to be watched over at my age, not that I mind."

"She delivers your meals?" Tension eased from Caylee's shoulders. Jett's visitor wasn't a girlfriend, but a relative who cared. All her worrying had been for nothing. If Jett were as trustworthy as he seemed, she just hoped she could trust herself.

Jett set down his fork and glanced at Caylee. "You up for dessert?"

"I don't think I could fit another bite into my stomach. It's full and perfectly content."

Jett's phone pinged an incoming message. The sounds of the restaurant faded into the background as he stared at his dad's text: *Congratulations on the new car. Ben's been keeping me in the loop. Proud of you, son. Love you.*

For a moment, Jett couldn't move. The words blurred on the screen. For years, he'd told himself his father didn't care. Years of silence, of believing he didn't matter, unraveled with those simple words.

The young dad at the next table wiped taco sauce from his son's cheek. Jett looked again at the text as memories tumbled through his mind. The way his dad patiently taught him to work on car and van engines, and showed him how to work on AC units. Another memory flashed of his dad standing in the kitchen the week after Mom died. Despite that, Dad made pancakes every Sunday morning just like Mom had done.

Jett blinked back the moisture building in his eyes. Fingers trembling, he typed back. *Thanks, Dad. Means a lot. Love u 2*

Caylee's hand brushed his. "Is everything okay?"

He took a deep breath and slowly exhaled, as though breathing out the lies and replacing them with the truth. The old ache eased, like a door he'd thought locked forever had cracked open.

"Better than okay." Jett took her hand in his. "I sent Dad a picture of the car. He texted back. Said he's proud of me."

"That's sweet."

"Yeah. We've barely spoken in years. I thought he didn't care. Turns out I might've been wrong."

Caylee's smile was soft, her eyes warm as she met Jett's gaze. "Sometimes it takes time to see clearly. I'm working on that too."

He turned his hand palm-up in hers, lacing their fingers. "I guess so. I'm ready to stop holding onto old hurts."

“Me too. My mom says clinging to regrets is like digging through the dumpster after you’ve already taken out the trash. Only gets you dirtier.”

“Looks like I’ve been living in that dumpster too long. Time to haul it to the curb.”

Caylee squeezed his fingers. “Maybe we can help each other climb out.”

“Sounds great.” Jett grinned at his beautiful date. For once, the future didn’t feel like something to dread. Maybe his dad never stopped loving, even if it was in ways Jett hadn’t noticed. And now he was sitting with a woman who saw him and cared, squirrels and all.

Chapter 14

Early sunshine flitted through the trees as Caylee walked the winding trail. Even though it was a Saturday morning, she'd gotten up early. Sleep had been impossible after Winthrop's late-night call, saying how he still loved and missed her.

Caylee kicked at a small rock. Why, after all this time, had he reached out? And worse, she'd felt that old, familiar tug toward Winthrop's charm. Why now, when she was enjoying being with Jett?

The rhythmic stride of another jogger approached from behind, and Caylee moved to the right. A tall, slender woman glided effortlessly by. Caylee's shoulders drew up, her body tensing. She'd never be built like that.

She kept at her slower pace until reaching the small waterfall. Standing at the edge of the stream, Caylee watched an ant, like a tiny explorer on a grand adventure, perched on a leaf floating in the water. The gentle current guided the leaf past smooth stones, carrying it farther away until it finally vanished around a bend.

Why couldn't she be that carefree? Why did she always feel caught in currents she couldn't control, instead of trusting God?

She slipped off her shoes and waded into the cool water. Settling on the big rock, she hugged her knees and gazed at the clouds drifting by.

Winthrop's calls echoed in her thoughts, a reminder of manipulation and her own repeated failures to walk away sooner.

She'd spent so much time replaying old hurts, wondering what she could have done differently, wishing she'd seen the red flags sooner. Caylee groaned. Why had she stayed with Winthrop all those years, and why had she kept returning to him? Why didn't she stand up to him sooner?

At least last night, she'd told him never to call her again, and she blocked his number.

Caylee stared up at the blue sky. "God, thank you for your forgiveness. Please help me forgive myself. I don't want to live trapped in guilt and regret anymore. Help me let it go so I can move forward."

Another leaf floated by, and Caylee imagined her regrets, washed clean by grace, drifting downstream. She let her feet dangle in the stream, the cool water swirling around her toes. Maybe forgiveness wasn't just about releasing the past, but making room for something new.

A squirrel darted across the opposite bank, then halted, its tail flicking. Caylee grinned, thinking of Jett and his ongoing battles with wildlife. Being with him was different. She didn't have to perform or pretend. She could just be herself. Be comfortable. Be okay with who she was.

Caylee stretched her legs, then stood and brushed off her shorts. Later today, Jett was taking her to a place he'd found up in the hills for a picnic.

She pushed off the rock. Her foot slid on moss, and she shifted her weight to steady herself. Taking another step, her little toe slammed into a sharp rock; the sting shot up her leg as if a tiny lightning bolt had zapped her. Fighting to keep from falling, her arms windmilled in wild circles. For one hopeful half-second, she thought she'd recovered. Then her other foot hit another slimy patch.

Traction gone and balance evaporated, she toppled backward, her arms flapping like a startled chicken.

She landed in the stream with a sploosh that sent water straight up her nose.

Sputtering and coughing, Caylee sat up in the shallow water, hair plastered across her forehead, shirt clinging in unflattering ways. To make matters worse, a leaf was stuck to her cheek like nature's beauty mark.

Muttering about her very ungraceful moves, she crawled toward the shore on hands and knees, mud sucking at her palms and streaking her shorts in artistic swirls that would make a toddler proud.

One knee slipped, and Caylee face-planted into the soft bank. Groaning, she swiped at her nose. Perfect. She was officially a mud monster. Turning back to the water, she scrubbed her face.

Flopping onto her back, she stared up at the puffy clouds. The absurdity hit her full force. Here she was, fresh from praying to move forward, and she'd been knocked down, dunked, muddied, and given a leaf facial.

Caylee burst out laughing as she raised her hands in triumph. Life might knock her down, but she could laugh like a crazy woman and keep going.

A shadow fell across her face. "You need to be careful lying there like that. Squirrels might get you."

Heat rocketing to her face, she jerked upright, swiped wet hair from her eyes, and stared into Jett's handsome face. "You should have been here to catch me."

"Wish I had," Jett knelt beside her, concern flickering in his gaze. "You okay?"

"Yes, I'm fine. But if you witnessed any of that, I'm completely mortified." Caylee tried to brush mud from her shirt, but only succeeded in smearing it further. Thank goodness the water hadn't made her t-shirt see-through.

"Nothing to be ashamed of. I thought you looked like a ballerina pirouetting in Swan Lake." He grinned and offered his hand.

She shoved her still-wet feet into her sneakers, grabbed hold of his fingers, and rose to her feet. "No swans here, and I'm definitely not coordinated enough for ballet. I'll stick to spreadsheets."

"Sorry I don't have a towel for you." Jett's voice was tinged with amusement.

Caylee raised an eyebrow and playfully narrowed her eyes. "What are you doing here, anyway?"

Jett leaned in close enough that she could smell the faint scent of coffee on his breath. "I could ask you the same question. This is *my* spot, you know. I found it first."

"Probably even before the pioneers, huh?" Failing to suppress her smile, she crossed her arms.

"Definitely." He snatched a nearby stick and drove it dramatically into the dirt with a solid thunk. "I, Jett Ryder, stake my claim on this spot on this day for now and forever."

"That's not how it works."

He mirrored her stance, muscles flexing under his t-shirt. "It's not?"

"No. Just ask them." Caylee pointed to two blackbirds perched on a nearby limb, their beady eyes staring at them like feathered judges.

Jett's gaze flicked to the tree, then back to her. "Take steady steps," he whispered, "and back away slowly before they attack." He reached for her hand. "I'll get you home safe."

She bit her lip to keep from laughing as Jett took exaggerated, slow-motion steps like a cartoon character sneaking past guards.

Caylee cracked up as Jett broke into a full run, tugging her behind him. Her wet sneakers squished with every step as they bobbed and weaved along the trail.

Jett skidded to a sudden stop.

Caylee smashed into his broad back.

He turned, their faces inches apart. "Can't keep your hands off me, can you?"

She tilted her head, giving him a saucy look. "Says the man who's still holding my hand."

His thumb brushed slowly over her knuckles, the touch light but electric against her skin. Jett's gaze dipped to her lips, lingering long enough to make her breathing difficult, before lifting to her eyes.

Jett cleared his throat. "Don't you have a hot date later?"

A nervous laugh slipped out, and Caylee straightened and tried to act more in control. "I do. But I'm not in a hurry. I have good intel that he's not at home right now."

"I have no doubt he'll be on time to pick you up." His voice softened, the teasing giving way to something more vulnerable.

He released her hand and took a small step back, though his eyes stayed locked on hers, as though reluctant to break the connection.

A tiny pang of disappointment flickered through Caylee, but was chased by gratitude that Jett was honoring the slow unfolding of whatever this was.

Still, part of her wanted to close the gap, but the wiser part whispered to be cautious. God had carried her regrets downstream; maybe He was guiding this new path just as carefully.

She tucked a damp strand of hair behind her ear. "Thanks for saving me again."

"Anytime," Jett offered his arm like an old-fashioned gentleman. "Come on, drowned ballerina. Let's get you home before those blackbirds send reinforcements."

She slipped her arm through his as their footsteps fell into sync. Today, she was not just moving forward. She was choosing joy, one muddy, squishy footprint at a time.

Chapter 15

At the spot he'd found for a picnic, Jett carefully lifted Caylee over the jagged barbed wire, easing her beside him onto the ground.

Her hands rested on his shoulders as her blue eyes gazed up at him. "Thank you, kind sir."

"My pleasure." Jett hated to release her, but he did. He hoisted the picnic basket onto his shoulder while Caylee gathered the checkered blanket against her chest.

The Smoky Mountains' blue-green ridges stretched before them as they walked side-by-side.

"It's beautiful here," Caylee said.

"I thought so, too. Found it on one of my service calls." Jett set the basket beneath a massive oak tree, then spread out the blanket.

Caylee smoothed the fabric and swiped away the grass and twigs before sitting down.

Placing the basket between them, he peeked inside. His mouth watered at the contents. "This will be great."

"You say that as though you didn't know what you brought."

"Well, I didn't exactly put it together."

Caylee puffed a laugh. "Don't tell me. Your cousin's wife provided the food."

He might as well be honest. "Yep, along with the basket and blanket. Tiffany was worried that I'd bring something like beef jerky, chips, and a couple of cans of soda."

Caylee shrugged and grinned. "Sounds okay to me."

"You are my kind of woman." He had no clue why someone as beautiful, kind, and fun as Caylee would have anything to do with him, but he sure was grateful.

Jett set the paper plates between them before bowing his head and thanking God for the food and the time they had together.

After the prayer, they ate in comfortable silence. The scenery and being with Caylee were enough.

She helped him clean up after the meal, then they stretched out on the soft blanket.

Lying next to him, she traced a cloud with her finger. "Looks like a penguin."

Jett squinted. "I see it." He pointed to another one. "Dragon."

"I don't think so. That has the look of a plucked chicken to me."

He glanced over at her. "Have you ever seen one in person?"

She turned her head toward him. "Yes, every time I go to the meat counter at the grocery store."

"Ha, ha, ha, miss smarty pants."

"Okay, what else do you see?"

Jett motioned to the cloud next to her idea of a plucked chicken. "That one looks like a dog."

"Okay, I'll give you that one. Did you have pets growing up?"

"Yeah," Jett rolled onto his side, propping his head on his hand. "We had a German Shepherd. He passed about a year after my mom died." He coughed to clear the lump forming in his throat. "I think the dog missed her even more than we did. He barely ate, barely wagged. Just kind of faded."

“Oh, Jett, I’m so sorry.” Caylee sat silent for a moment as though she understood his need to process. “I had a gerbil named Gerty for a few years. It was hard enough to lose him. I can’t imagine a family dog.”

“Yeah, death is the pits.” Not wanting to spoil the mood, Jett shifted to a seated position and gestured toward the mountains. “Can you imagine how quiet it would have been when people first lived here?”

She sat next to him, her shoulder touching his. “Life was probably so peaceful without cars, planes, and machines. Just the gentle sounds of nature.”

Jett tried to keep the grin off his face. “Other than the occasional person falling into a stream.”

Caylee smirked. “Or men running through the forest while being attacked by squirrels.”

“Maybe pioneer life wasn’t for us.”

“I don’t know. It would’ve been great, as long as there was a grocery store and online shopping.”

Jett nudged her shoulder. “Sounds like Garden Valley.”

“Yes, it does.” Caylee nudged him back. “Are you glad you moved here?”

“I am. It’s not where I thought I’d be, but I’m grateful God brought me here.” He looked over at his beautiful friend.

“I’m glad you came. Otherwise, I’d still be permanently frozen at my desk.”

Jett raised an eyebrow. “Your napkin and folder accessories did give you an interesting look.”

A blush spread across her cheeks. “I’m glad it didn’t keep you from texting me.”

“I had to make sure you were safe from wandering penguins.”

Caylee’s eyes widened as she pointed behind him.

Jett chuckled. "Penguin attack?"

"No," she whispered. "Massive cow heading straight for us."

Jett whipped his head around—and froze. The largest bull he'd ever seen was coming their way. The enormous horns and black hide glistened in the sun as the animal ambled toward them. Jett's stomach dropped. He should have realized this field could be used for grazing land.

He grabbed the blanket just as Caylee did, and the red checkered fabric waved like a bullfighter's cape in the breeze. Jett yanked it free, shoved the blanket inside, then stepped in front of Caylee and backed them away. "Move slow. No sudden moves. I'll stay in front to block the attack."

Caylee's heart slammed against her ribs as the bull huffed, lowered its massive head, and picked up its pace. The fence was only a few yards behind them, but the bull was closing the distance fast.

Whimpering, she fisted the back of Jett's t-shirt as they backpedaled toward the fence. "Why couldn't it be a squirrel?"

"If he charges," he said quietly, "promise me you'll run."

"Run?" Her voice wobbled. "I'll be moving in jet mode. Do angry bulls look like this, or should smoke come out of their noses before they gore their victims?"

"Let's not find out." Jett hustled Caylee back to the fence, dropped the basket, and hoisted her over the wires in one smooth motion.

She hit the ground on the other side, spun around as the bull broke into a full charge. "Jett! Hurry."

He shoved the basket at her and vaulted. The barbed wire caught his jeans. He grunted, twisting, the fence rattling as the bull thundered closer.

Caylee ripped open the basket, grabbed the first thing her fingers closed around, and hurled a sandwich with every ounce of panic-fueled strength she had.

Smack.

The sandwich hit the bull square between the horns. Lettuce exploded. Bread, meat, and Mayo slid down his face.

The bull skidded to a halt, snorted, shook its massive head, then charged toward them with renewed speed.

Jett yanked free, his jeans ripping, and hit the ground hard just as the bull slammed into the fence.

The wire strained, and the posts creaked in protest, but held tight. With a deep, furious bellow, the massive animal shook its head, turned, and lumbered away.

Jett crossed the distance in two strides and crushed Caylee against him. "If anything had happened—" His voice broke.

"Hey, it didn't." She pressed her cheek against his still racing heart. "We're safe."

His grip tightened. "I shouldn't have put you in danger."

"Oh, Jett." She leaned back just enough to look at him. "You didn't know. That bull may have come from anywhere."

"I'm supposed to protect you."

Caylee's lip trembled at his sweetness. "You did." She kissed his cheek. "You always do." Winthrop would have tripped her so that he could get away.

Emotions flickered across his face, then he softly pressed his lips against hers.

Still buzzing with adrenaline, Caylee kissed him back with gusto.

Jett groaned, then pulled away, threading his fingers through hers. "Come on, let's get you home."

Caylee leaned against him as they walked toward his car. She'd never known anyone like Jett.

She slid into the seat and waited until he got behind the wheel, then pointed to his ripped jeans. "We really need to find less exciting ways to spend time together. How about Monday night, I cook you a nice, quiet dinner at my place?"

"Yeah, safer that way." Jett stared straight ahead as he started his car.

Caylee rested her hand on his arm. "You saved me again."

Jett still didn't look at her. "No, I didn't." He shook his head. "You're too good for me."

What was he thinking? She was a mess. She swatted his shoulder. "Oh, no, you don't. Do *not* get all poor me on me. I do enough of that for both of us. I had a wonderful time. I always do when we're together. You're fun, handsome, sweet, and we get to have the most incredible adventures. And I want them to continue."

Jett sat still, then huffed out a quiet breath and turned toward her. "You are the most amazing woman I've ever met."

"Obviously, you don't get out much. But I'll take it. Now let's get back to the apartments and enjoy more kisses."

He let out a chuckle. "I can't believe you threw a sandwich at a charging bull."

"Hey, it probably gave you at least two seconds more than you would have had."

Jett grinned. "Probably so." He floored the car. Gravel pinged and scattered behind as it surged forward.

Laughing, Caylee rolled down her window and let the air flow through, washing away life's worries. Jett Ryder had definitely become her favorite adventure.

Chapter 16

"I do not understand why you're complaining,

Caylee huffed out a breath as she walked next to Amy after lunch. "Seriously?" Caylee side-stepped a couple talking in the hallway. "Nothing weird, strange, or life-threatening has happened with Jett and me for the last three months, five days," she paused and checked the time, "and two hours."

Amy opened the door for them. "Sounds like things are going well."

"It's complicated." Caylee entered her cubicle and dropped into her chair. "We've attended church together, played video games with you and Quint, gone on long walks, and taken scenic drives in the country. I've cooked meals, and we've gone out to eat. We've even hiked for miles on the Appalachian Trail."

"Sounds perfect to me."

"It is. Jett's wonderful. I have never had a better time with anyone in my life."

Amy leaned against the cubicle wall. "I am *not* following you."

Caylee fingered the stack of folders on her desk. "I don't deserve him, Amy. The more time we spend together, the more I love him and the more worried I am that he will see through me and find out I'm nothing special."

"Love?" Amy grinned. "Have you told Jett you love him?"

"Of course not," Caylee stared at the smiling photo of Jett on her desk. "Not out loud, anyway."

"Has Jett said the words?"

The clack of keyboards and the banter from the ladies in the next cubicle were familiar and usually comforting, but not now. "Yes, he's said it several times," Caylee murmured.

Amy pushed off the cubicle wall. "Oh, my goodness! Why didn't you tell me?"

"I don't know. It just didn't seem right since I didn't say it back."

Amy's smile faltered as she studied Caylee. "Why do you think you're nothing special? You're smart, funny, beautiful, and a great friend to your great friend," Amy pointed to herself. "What are you so worried about?"

Caylee looked away. She wasn't even sure herself. Winthrop had told her he loved her, and she'd jumped right into that love thing without a second thought. But saying the words back hadn't helped the relationship. They'd only trapped her.

"Wait, you're not living a secret life, are you? I know. You're a fugitive from another country because you consumed that entire nation's strategic chocolate reserve. And now their CIA is after you. That's the chocolate indulgence agency."

Caylee rolled her eyes. "It's nothing like that. I'm paranoid that something bad will happen because everything is going so well."

"Well, that's a serious waste of time."

"I know it is. But my brain is in a swirling, twirling mess of worries, and I can't figure out how to get out of the hurricane."

Amy sat motionless, just staring at her, then leaned close. "Who are you and what have you done with my normally level-headed friend?"

Caylee shifted in her chair. "I don't know," she whimpered.

Amy's eyes narrowed. "Has Jett said or done something that made your head get into this spiraling vortex?"

“No, he’s wonderful.” Caylee pinched the bridge of her nose, trying to stop those annoying tears from forming.

“Okaaaaay,” Amy tilted her head. “Has Winjerk called again?”

“No, I blocked him, remember? He’s left me alone.”

“Good. So, have you researched what started the brain twirls?”

“I don’t know.” Caylee stared at her computer screen, the numbers blurring in front of her. “It just crept up on me and pounced.”

Amy tapped her chin with her finger for a moment. “Well, I think I know how to stop your worries.” She sat in the chair next to Caylee and scooted close. “You’ve been worried about something bad happening, not realizing all the time that your worries are bad.”

Caylee stared at her friend, trying to process what she’d shared.

“So,” Amy continued, “you don’t need to worry anymore because the good got messed up by the bad. So, the bad thing you were worried about already happened.”

Caylee puffed out a laugh. “That is a unique way of looking at things.”

“Makes sense to me. Besides that, God’s got you covered.”

Caylee leaned back in her chair. Was she so worried about a bad thing happening that the bad thing was the worrying? Once again, it came back to trusting God, letting go of the past, and refusing to worry about the future. She sat thinking and praying. The tension in her shoulders eased. As though rising above the hurricane vortex, her thoughts began to settle.

Amy stood and held out her hand. “That will be twelve hundred dollars for my consultation or two pieces out of your chocolate stash.”

Caylee rummaged through her bottom desk drawer, where she hid her sweet supplies, and handed her friend three pieces. "You're worth it."

"It's going to be okay." Amy hugged her. "You can enjoy the journey. Worries will come, just don't invite them in to stay."

After her friend left, Caylee picked up Jett's photo she'd taken on one of their hikes. Wearing jeans, a t-shirt, and hiking boots, he leaned against a split-rail fence. That day was the first time he told her he loved her.

And she'd said nothing, just held him close and kissed him, hoping that her feelings would show in her actions. She could tell he noticed, and yet he continued to tell her he loved her.

Her worries were lifting, but why couldn't she tell Jett how she really felt?

Jett removed the panels on the outdoor unit and cleaned the condenser coil. Fortunately, the homeowner had kept plants clear of the unit to provide adequate airspace.

He inspected the fan blade, motor, and capacitor. Everything looked good. He hadn't been worried about this call since regular service checks for customers usually went well.

Jett finished and put his tools in the van. He knocked on the door to let the customer know he was finished.

"Thank you so much for doing that for me," the white-haired lady he'd seen at church motioned him inside. "Can I get you a bottle of water?"

"Yes, ma'am. Thank you." Jett usually brought a cooler with him with bottled water, but today he'd been distracted.

He loved Caylee, and he thought she felt the same way, but she never said she loved him. At first, he thought he'd rushed saying the words, but now he wondered if her feelings weren't the same as his.

Jett stood waiting in the lady's family room. Family photos lined the fireplace mantle, his attention drawn to a picture of a smiling couple standing with a boy in a soccer uniform. Jett rubbed the ache in his chest.

"That's my son and his family." The lady handed Jett the water. "My grandson is great at soccer, but last month he broke his leg. We're not sure if he'll play again. We will all be disappointed if he doesn't, but if not, God will have something else for him."

"Yes, ma'am. I'm sure he'll be fine." Jett twisted off the bottle cap and took a swig of the chilly water as he stared at the framed photo. The smiling boy stood between his parents, shin guards too large, one small hand clutching a grass-stained ball.

Jett's throat tightened, the familiar ache pressing deeper than he expected. All those years, he'd read his dad's silences as blame for the hit that stopped his heart, for having to quit the one thing that had made them close.

But now the pieces shifted. Maybe his dad's clipped words hadn't been anger at Jett, but grief. For the son who'd flatlined under stadium lights, for the Saturdays that turned empty, for a future stolen in one brutal second. His dad may have been devastated—not with him, but for him.

"Are you married?"

Jett blinked to clear his vision, then shook his head. "No ma'am. Not yet."

"Sounds like you have someone in mind."

The thought of Caylee brought him back to the present. "I do. Just not sure she feels the same way."

The lady patted his arm. "Give her time. And pray for God's guidance. You want God's best for you both."

"Thank you, ma'am. I'd better get back to work."

She glanced at his shirt, then back to his face. "Jett, I will pray for you and your young lady."

"I appreciate that."

Jett drove to his next service call. He prayed for Caylee, and he'd been praying that she would love him too. But he hadn't been praying for her best or for his.

He glanced up at the sky for a moment. It was time to change his prayers and trust God for the outcome, but he really, really hoped they were on the same page.

Chapter 17

After work, Caylee drove toward her apartment, rehearsing how she would tell Jett that she loved him. Out loud this time, not just in smiles and kisses.

Hopefully, he would say it first, and she could respond without overthinking. If not, she could casually slip it into a conversation.

The plan for the evening was to eat at the bistro in town, then come back to her place and play backgammon. Jett won most of the time, but tonight she just knew she could be victorious, especially if she told Jett she loved him while they were playing the game.

She pulled into her apartment's parking lot and hurried inside. She wanted to get a shower and change into something that would catch Jett's attention. Nothing showy or inappropriate. Just her.

Her phone rang.

"Hey, Mom. What's up?" Caylee stood in her bedroom, looking into her closet to choose something to wear.

"Honey, I need you to come home."

Caylee clenched the phone. "Is everything okay?"

"Yes, we're fine, but there's someone here. It's Winthrop," she whispered.

Caylee wanted to scream. Why would he be at their house? How dare he bother her sweet parents. "I'll be right there." The quicker she got there, the sooner she could tell him to leave and never come back.

Driving the winding roads, Caylee prayed, asking God why Winthrop was in the area and why He'd let him near her again. She should never have let him know where she'd moved. At least he didn't know she had her own apartment now.

She slowed her speed at the upcoming sharp curve. Her thoughts went to Jett and his tender ways.

Caylee smacked the steering wheel. The nerve of Winthrop showing up after she'd blocked him. No wonder she had been in that worry vortex. It was probably a heavenly warning that trouble was brewing.

She parked in her parents' driveway behind Winthrop's black Porsche 911 Carrera GTS. She knew the make and model and the price since Winthrop bragged about it so much.

Caylee took a deep breath and entered through the back door. The sound of his deep voice, along with her mom's, mingled from the family room.

She stepped into the room. Her dad, broom in hand, swept at the clean hardwood floor while sending scathing looks in Winthrop's direction, while her mom sat on the couch in polite but obviously uncomfortable conversation.

Winthrop, tall and handsome as ever, rose the moment he saw her and wrapped his arms around her. "I've missed you, baby."

Caylee pushed away, her hands firm against his chest. "What are you doing here?"

Surprise flickered across his face before his assured smile slid back into place. "I was worried when I couldn't get a hold of you."

She met his gaze without flinching. "I blocked you."

His eyes narrowed for the briefest second, cold and assessing, then softened as if he'd rehearsed the expression in the mirror. "I can't believe you'd do this to me." He took her hand in his manicured one. "You know I love you."

Caylee pulled back. "You don't love me."

Winthrop glanced at her parents as though they would agree with him. "Yes, I do. I just didn't realize how much."

He stepped closer. "Come with me to Switzerland."

"No, Winthrop. It's over."

Her parents glared at Winthrop. Caylee sent them a nod, a silent okay, not to worry. Her dad muttered something about not liking controlling guys, and her mom patted Caylee's arm as they left the room.

Winthrop's jaw tensed before he took on that familiar, charming look he did so well. "It's not over." He reached into his pocket, pulled out a small velvet box, dropped to one knee, and held it toward her. A large, marquise-cut diamond sparkled in the light, trying to mesmerize her into submission.

"Caylee Ann Timmons, marry me."

Once, that ring would have stolen her breath. Now, it meant nothing. She straightened and kept her voice calm. "No, Winthrop. I won't ever marry you."

His smile faltered. "Of course you'll marry me. This is what you wanted. *I'm* what you want."

She took a small step back, not in fear, but in confidence. "The answer is no and will always be no."

Winthrop snapped the box shut, stood, and leaned into her face. His eyes flashed with cold fury; his lips pressed into a thin, furious line. "You're making a mistake, Caylee. I could give you *everything* your heart desired."

"No, you couldn't. Only God can do that. You need to leave and never come back."

Finished for the day, Jett stared at Caylee's text. She'd canceled their date.

He shoved his phone into his back pocket. He had prayed for Caylee's best.

Was God's answer that her best was for him to let her go?

Chapter 18

Wind rushing through the open car window, Caylee cranked up the radio and sang at the top of her lungs. She didn't care how awful she sounded. She laughed, finally feeling free.

Winthrop was behind her now. No longer tugging at her heart. Not whispering lies disguised as love.

"Thank You, Lord!" she shouted.

Being away from Winthrop and closer to God had shown her the truth. She wasn't broken. She wasn't unworthy. God's love was enough.

And Jett... She grinned, gripping the steering wheel. She couldn't wait to tell him she loved him.

He was different; the way he listened, prayed, and stepped between her and danger without hesitation. Even more, the way he loved without conditions or manipulation.

Caylee slowed to take a curve. She didn't deserve God's love or the love of a good man, but God had always been kinder than she ever expected. If Jett was a gift from God, she wanted to steward that gift well. Cherish the moments. Keep focused on God and try to live in a way that regrets wouldn't haunt her anymore.

She pulled into the parking lot, hurried to Jett's apartment, and knocked.

No answer.

She sent him a text.

Nothing.

Where was he? Taking two steps at a time, she ran to check the fitness room and laundry area. He wasn't there either.

Jett's Mustang sat tucked beneath its cover. He had to be here.

Lightning flickered in the distance. A low roll of thunder followed. A tightness crept into Caylee's chest.

She called his phone. "Jett, it's me. Please call me."

The wind whipped around her, warning of an upcoming storm. Had she hesitated one too many times to tell him she loved him?

The thought took her breath. *No. Please, no.*

She rubbed her forehead, trying to think. Could he have gone to the trail?

Caylee hurried inside her apartment, quickly changed, and found her only flashlight. It wasn't too bright, but hopefully it would help her find her way. She rushed back down the stairs.

"Please be there," she whispered as she broke into a run.

Jett sat by the stream. A bird shrilled in the distance. Crickets chirped in a steady rhythm.

He'd come here to do the right thing. No matter how much he loved Caylee, he needed to trust God with her.

"If her best isn't me," Jett whispered, "give me the strength to step aside."

Thunder rolled in the distance as though giving him an answer.

Jett didn't move as he let go of the picture he'd been carrying in his heart of him and Caylee together as man and wife.

Rain slicked his skin, raindrop tears mingling with his own as he released the only woman he'd ever loved.

Jett pressed his hand against his chest, the ache growing, not easing.

A light flashed through the trees.

The beam sliced closer, cutting through the rain. "Jett?"

"Caylee?" Had he imagined hearing her voice?

She called again, and he stood too fast, nearly losing his footing.

Caylee burst into the clearing, breathless and rain-soaked, her flashlight shaking in her hand. She stopped in front of him, chest heaving. "Jett Ryder, I love you. I've loved you for a long time. I was just afraid to say it."

He stared at her, the world narrowing to the sound of rain and his own heartbeat. "You canceled our date," the words came out hoarse. "I thought—"

"I know." She stepped closer, her wet fingers curling into his shirt. "Winthrop came back. He proposed."

Jett groaned. He knew it was too good to be true.

Rain fell harder now, soaking them both.

"I said no," Caylee's grip tightened on his shirt. "I need to trust God with my heart and trust you. I finally know who I am, and Who I belong to." She lifted her gaze to the storm-filled sky before turning back to him. "And I needed to tell the man I love. I'm choosing you, Jett. If you'll have me."

He exhaled a breath he didn't realize he'd been holding. She'd chosen *him.* Unsure if he could believe his ears, he wrapped his hand around hers. "Yes, Caylee. I choose you, too. I love you, and I promise I'll be here for you, no matter what."

She laughed through tears. "That is a wonderful promise, with all the craziness we've been through."

Laughing along with Caylee, Jett pulled her into his arms as the rain poured down around them, certain now that God had answered, not with thunder, but with the woman he loved.

Epilogue

The buzz of technology in the AI department filled the air as Caylee peered over Quint's shoulder. "This will either be the sweetest or the strangest surprise ever."

"Probably both." Amy grinned from her perch on a nearby ergonomic stool. "But it's a great way to celebrate your first wedding anniversary."

Quint's fingers danced across his keyboard with practiced speed, the soft click-clack punctuating the background drone of distant 3D printers whirring in the corner. "SAUS is more than happy to help. However, I can honestly say this is the first time anyone's asked me to program an AI video starring squirrels."

Caylee playfully narrowed her eyes. "I knew you'd be up for it. Especially since you two put a squirrel and a penguin on our wedding cake instead of a bride and groom."

Amy snorted. "I wish you could have seen your face."

Caylee laughed, remembering the joy of the day she became Jett's wife. "It was a cute surprise."

"So," Quint asked as he gave her a questioning glance, "you want the animals to take credit for your love story?"

"Yes, then they can congratulate us on our anniversary."

Quint worked several more minutes. At the soft beep of a successful render preview, he tapped the screen. "How's this looking?"

Caylee burst out laughing. "That is perfect. How should I have them make the next announcement?"

Quint held up his hand. "No worries, I've got it."

After dinner that night, Caylee gave a contented sigh as she glanced over from the passenger seat while Jett drove his Mustang down the winding driveway. Lamplight glowed from the front window of their house, nestled in the hills near Garden Valley.

She grinned at her sweet husband. "Dinner was so good."

"It really was. Best steak I've had in years." Jett parked in the garage and hurried to help her out. "I still can't believe we could afford something this nice."

Caylee took his hand. "The money your dad gave us as a wedding gift was a tremendous help. I'm so glad you two are close again."

"Me too. God's blessings just keep coming, don't they?" Jett followed her into the family room.

She could barely hide her excitement as she picked up the remote and sat on the couch. "I have something to show you."

Jett dropped next to her. "If this is another squirrel video, I'm officially filing a complaint."

She just smiled and pressed play.

Soft music played as a plump, gray squirrel with enormous eyes and a ridiculously fluffy tail zoomed into the frame astride a tiny but detailed motorcycle. The squirrel was outfitted in a sleek black leather jacket complete with armored-looking panels, a matte-black helmet with the visor pushed up, and a tough backpack slung over one shoulder.

"Yep, that was me." The squirrel's chipper, slightly squeaky voice declared. "I dashed across the road and caused the swerve of destiny. You're welcome, lovebirds."

Jett laughed. "That's great."

A penguin wearing a parka waddled on-screen. "The office was cold, but it led to a warm love."

Then another squirrel in a crisp HVAC shirt with the company logo on the front pocket appeared. "And don't forget that I had built the coziest nest ever until this guy poked around," he jabbed his paw toward them. "However, you, Jett Ryder, were kind to save my nest." He placed a paw on his chest. "My family thanks you."

A cartoon bull emerged, snorting and stomping its hooves, before offering a wide grin. "Glad my charge helped you two out."

The bull, penguin, along with a group of squirrels in their natural fluff, lined up, bushy tails waving. "Happy first wedding anniversary, Caylee and Jett!"

Grinning widely, Biker Squirrel took a small bow. "We, the heroic animals of fate, celebrate your epic love story. From daring road rescues...."

"To better temperatures." The penguin added, tossing its parka into the air.

The HVAC Squirrel made a heart sign. "To home nest saves."

The bull bowed. "And destiny charges."

They linked paws, hooves, and flippers. "We are part of God's amazing plan." They took a bow, then paused.

Biker squirrel cleared his throat with an exaggerated cough, fluffing his tail dramatically. "Also, we'd like to announce that our work here is not done."

Tiny hearts rained down across the screen. The music swelled as the next frame showed a baby squirrel waving a tiny paw.

The animals cheered, "Congratulations, Jett, on becoming a father!"

Jett stared at the screen, then his gaze whipped toward Caylee. "A baby?" His voice cracked. "You... me... a baby?"

"Yes," tears blurring her vision, she whispered. "You're going to be a daddy."

For a long moment, Jett didn't speak. He stared at the screen, then at her.

Breathless laughter bubbled out of him as he wrapped his arms around her and lifted her off her feet, holding her close. "Caylee, this is amazing. God can use anything, can't he? Even squirrels, penguins, and bulls."

"Yes," Caylee laughed. "You know we didn't get here because everything went right."

Jett pressed a kiss to her forehead. "We got here because God didn't give up on us."

"And neither did love." She kissed her sweet husband with a promise of another chapter of the breathtaking adventure God had written just for them.

The End

Thank you for reading

Squirrels, Spreadsheets, and the Courage to Trust

If you enjoyed the story, I'd be incredibly grateful if you'd take a moment to leave a review on Amazon.

Even a brief note or star rating helps other readers discover the story and would mean the world to me. Caylee, Jett, and the squirrels would also be grateful.

Lisa's Amazon page https://amzn.to/4ltfEBA

Visit Lisa's website https://lisabuffaloe.com
Facebook https://facebook.com/lisabuffaloe
Twitter (X) https://x.com/lisabuffaloe
Instagram https://instagram.com/buffaloelisa

Also by Lisa Buffaloe

Garden Valley, TN Series

Clues, Crushes, and Second Chances

Cook, Code, and a Leap of Faith

Squirrels, Spreadsheets, and the Courage to Trust

Crawdad Beach Series

Visible, yet Hidden

Running to Grace

Crystal's Journey Home

A Baker's Heart

Stella's Heart Code

River Steps Free

Mia Lets Go

A New Paige

Running from Shame

Elise's New Song

A Found Joy

A Healing Rain

Hope and Grace Series

Nadia's Hope

Prodigal Nights

The Discovery Chapter

Open Lens

Writing Her Heart

Stand-alone novels

The Masterpiece Beneath

The Fortune

Grace for the Char-Baked

Non-Fiction

Finding Freedom in a Binding World
Float by Faith
Heart and Soul Medication
Time with The Timeless One
The Forgotten Resting Place
Present in His Presence
We Were Meant for Paradise
One Lit Step: Devotions for your journey
The Unnamed Devotional
Flying on His Wings
Unfailing Treasures
No Wound Too Deep For The Deep Love of Christ
Living Joyfully Free Devotional (Volumes 1 & 2)

About the Author

Lisa Buffaloe is a happily married mom, multi-published author, and speaker who writes encouraging non-fiction and inspirational fiction ranging from touching women's fiction to light-hearted Christian rom-coms.

Drawing from her own journey of faith and freedom, she writes to encourage hearts and point readers toward the One who redeems every story.

No matter the scars from the past or challenges in the present, Lisa's books remind readers that God's grace brings healing, restoration, renewal, and true joy.

When she's not writing, you'll find her cherishing time with her husband, exploring God's breathtaking creation, or laughing over a good cup of coffee.

Acknowledgements

First off, I am so grateful for our forgiving, redeeming God who loves us through every wild and crazy time of our lives.

Heavenly Father, thank You especially for the tremendous gift of salvation that You grant through Your Son, Jesus Christ. Thank You for the sweet stories You have blessed me to write. May they bring honor and glory to Your name.

Dennis, thank you for being a loving, wonderful husband. Thank you for your prayers, support, and encouragement. I sure am grateful we are together.

Thank you, Patricia (Pacjac) Carroll, for your helpful feedback and for making the writing process so enjoyable.

JoAnn Durgin, thank you for creating another beautiful cover. You are a sweet blessing to me and so many others.

A big thanks to the squirrels who were furious when our roofers closed up the mushroom vent you used for access. Thank you for providing a fun scene for Jett.

God really does cause all things to work together for good to those who love God and are called according to His purpose (Romans 8:28).

Squirrels, Spreadsheets, and the Courage to Trust

Lisa Buffaloe

www.ingramcontent.com/pod-product-compliance
Lightning Source LLC
LaVergne TN
LVHW011029110826
845149LV00015B/3344

* 9 7 8 1 9 5 7 7 1 5 6 5 0 *